KRISTE

Night
A NOVEL
Street

GOOSE LANE

First published in Australia in 2010 by Allen & Unwin Pty Ltd.

Cover images: *Wet Evening* (detail), c. 1927, by Clarice Beckett, courtesy of Castlemaine Art Gallery and Historical Museum, Victoria, Australia, www.castlemainegallery.com; and *A sigh is just a sigh*, ~BostonBill~, flickr.com.
Cover design by Julie Scriver.
Page design by Post Pre-press Group, Australia.
Printed in Canada.
10 9 8 7 6 5 4 3 2 1

Library and Archives Canada Cataloguing in Publication

Thornell, Kristel
Night street / Kristel Thornell.

Issued also in electronic format.
ISBN 978-0-86492-672-2

1. Beckett, Clarice, 1887-1935 — Fiction. I. Title.

PR9619.4.T497N55 2012   823'.92   C2011-907808-2

Goose Lane Editions acknowledges the financial support of the Canada Council for the Arts, the Government of Canada through the Canada Book Fund (CBF), and the Government of New Brunswick through the Department of Wellness, Culture, and Sport.

Goose Lane Editions
500 Beaverbrook Court, Suite 330
Fredericton, New Brunswick
CANADA E3B 5X4
www.gooselane.com

FSC
www.fsc.org
MIX
Paper from
responsible sources
FSC® C016245

In respectful acknowledgement of Clarice Beckett, whose art and life drew me into this dream.

To be alone seems at once so natural and yet so un-natural I've never understood it.

Daniel Keene, *Two Shanks*

Night was approaching, cool tattered mist blowing in from the bay. She appeared in an area of transparent air, drawing along a wheeled object the size of a largish dog. From a distance, she made a perplexing spectacle, seeming slightly misshapen, some hybrid creature. Getting the contraption onto the beach was not so awkward, the tide having retreated to leave the sand compact and smooth. She pulled the thing, stopping, and pulling again, in search of the right position.

Out alone in the lowering light, with just the company of her equipment, she was at ease and people could stare if they wanted to. There were few people on the winter beach at that time, in any case. The only hardy or unusual enough were a solitary-looking man in a battered hat and a trio of fishermen accustomed to her presence. She waved to these unsociably, keeping her mind for herself, guarding it. Ceremonial, she was taking her time. She had an image of herself moving through the waning silvery twilight in her dowdy skirt and cardigan—but it was flickering, uncertain;

1

she was already losing track of who she was, of Clarice. The marine air was potent with the odour of kelp, between life and decomposition.

When she had chosen the spot, the purpose of her inanimate companion was revealed; a lid was lifted and treasures removed from its belly. Then the no-nonsense business of preparing the palette, and a wash was done in umber and next a brush had begun to pursue the colour of the moment: the unsettling, yielding blue of that precise evening's gravitation to darkness. She worked quickly, because she preferred it so and time was always short. Almost instantly, she fell into the self-hypnosis that resembles dream-filled sleep but is in fact a ruthless wakefulness. This was like a game. And so very serious.

She stepped back, at last. A simple scene. So deceptively bare that most would see nothing there. A curve of flat, open bay draped in dwindling radiance. The horizon line, barely perceptible, joining the two blue-mauve masses of sky and gently undulating sea. Everything soft, softening. Nightfall. The borderland time, neither here nor there, when the world, though seen less exactly, is more fully felt. The hazy edges made this scene appear malleable. Liable to change.

Clarice took another step back from her easel, and mist dropped like a fine curtain into the gap between the artist and the painted view, hiding it. Her figure, too, became confused with the mist shrouding the beach like unearthly smoke.

ONE
Open Air

1

She was already thirty and beginning to think of herself, with intermittent irony or embarrassment, as an artist, when she first heard Meldrum speak. An odd feeling of prescience told her he would influence her life. It turned out that he was the closest she would come to the tantalising world of European art, despite his decision to bring no reproductions back from abroad. He abhorred the avant-garde, rejecting even the Impressionists, but did show his class the copies he had made of artists such as Corot, Turner and Chardin. She would always love him for that. And possibly hate him a little, too, as you do when a person seems to have lifted off the top of your head, reached in and plucked out some of your choicest fantasies, then brazenly passed them off as someone else's.

Meldrum gave her permission to trust what she saw, discounting what did not strike her as important. Perhaps this was the same as saying that he allowed her to consider herself sane: if she was looking properly, she could take what she saw seriously, without suspecting herself caught in a net of private delusion. No small matter. He believed absolutely in sight, believed that by faithfully recording the impressions received by the eye, in the order of tone, proportion and colour, painting could render an accurate, scientifically constructed illusion of reality.

Tones came first. Apt and beautiful, the word *tone* for describing the stages of intensity of light and shade, gradations in luminosity being indeed every bit as subtle and sliding as the moods of a voice.

The lecture Meldrum presented that day to the Victorian Artists' Society was on his controversial, scientific approach to art. The man was as forceful as the ideas he was expounding. Meldrum was blatantly seduced by his own sober charisma; he represented an original, compelling ideal and you could not risk closing your eyes to it. Of course, the mythology surrounding him could not have been what it was had he himself not been a great believer in it. He was fabulously authoritative, splendidly convincing.

Without being tall or particularly robust, Meldrum was imposing in his black suit. In his early forties, he seemed barely middle-aged in nineteen seventeen and it was clear he was to be a significant player on the stage of Melbourne art. His pointed, still-dark beard, long, strong nose and close-set, probing eyes showed that he was a man of Reason. Waving his arms about behind a lectern (he might have picked up this loquacious gesturing during his French years or from his Gallic wife), he was like some Noah prophesying the flood, striving to convince a herd of backward, indolent animals to accompany him to salvation. He talked down to you from the height of his certainty, his intellectual and therefore moral righteousness; curiously, the effect was of a very sombre kind of sweet-talking, leaving you intent on embarking for whatever destination he was setting off for, signing up, enlisting in that pacifist's company. There were those who judged him harshly for his unmanly stance in relation to the war, but Meldrum was the hero of a different, equally vivid adventure. Art was a deadly important cause to which one could give oneself honourably. Clarice agreed with him.

Not quite naming the National Gallery School where he himself had got his start, Meldrum insinuated, with the force of his fierce freethinking logic, his low opinion of airless, fossilised, academic teaching and mentioned in passing that he had his own art school. By the end of that hour in the crammed hall fidgety with excitement, she had decided she was going to desert the Gallery School for his. She had completed her three years in drawing, once winning second prize, and been offered a place for a fourth in oil painting. She had intended on accepting it—until now. Alongside the apparition of this uncommonly impassioned Melbourne Scotsman, the prospect of the Gallery School, with its plodding rigidity, suddenly turned stolid, stifling: she had to be Meldrum's student.

For how long would she study with him? A year? She suspected that most of what she had to learn, she would have to teach herself. This was no doubt the case with everything.

2

When Meldrum finally noticed Clarice, truly registered her existence, she had been attending his Saturday afternoon class at the Hardware Chambers in Elizabeth Street for nearly a month.

Each week, after the instruction was over, he would use the final part of the class to make a round of the students, pronouncing on the paintings they had brought along, hopefully, timorously, for his critique. She happened to be the last for him to get to that day, and the lesson had just ended. There was a swift exodus, a rushing-off of students back to their less artistic lives, the few girls screening the daring lustre in their eyes with insouciance; most of them were alternately animated and insecure. Now only Meldrum, Clarice and Ada were left. Ada was shadowing Clarice, and clearly wanted the two of them to be friends, though Clarice was not drawn to form anything but a light alliance.

'I've already seen your work,' Meldrum told Ada, efficiently dismissing her. He was not worried about giving offence; his sense of purpose did not allow it. 'I'll speak with Clarice now.'

With a darting look at Clarice, Ada hurried to be gone.

And they were alone: the great teacher, his new pupil and her two small panels. Meldrum was somewhat subdued, having worn himself out rhapsodising about Velázquez.

'Let's see,' he said.

Quavering but feeling also queerly disembodied, Clarice laid them alongside one another on her easel, a still life and a landscape. It was the first time she had brought Meldrum a landscape. The decision to do so was a little rebellious, a slight provocation, because he maintained that students should stick to indoor work for at least two years before earning the right to take on wily natural light. But her interest in light's slipperiness was stubborn; it was a difficulty she wanted to be equal to.

Meldrum's eyes flicked over the landscape, did a double take and retreated to the still life, as if the first painting could be ignored.

'Hmm.'

He took two steps back, two more and another two, and settled his chin in the V of his right hand. He went rigid with concentration. The wise man pondering. Some small though strangely spacious amount of time passed. Then he shifted, coming in very close to the painting and scrutinising its surface, coldly analytical.

The still life was one of few she had completed that came close to satisfying her; generally she wanted to escape from interiors as fast as possible and be out in the open air, in real limitless space and tempting, fickle light. However, this was not, she hoped, uninteresting. It was not neatly domestic, not obvious, though the little assortment of objects she had portrayed was common enough. A vase of ranunculi, a glass bottle, an empty oriental vase, a string of coral beads. The flowers were sanguine and yellow, their dark centres echoing the almost-black background. The transparency of the glass was like a watery phantasmagorical after-image.

But the eye was drawn to the coral beads.

Meldrum made a tentative sound of approbation, but then produced another sound, shorter, higher.

In the foreground, the beads were familiar, recognisable as beads, yet also startling. Their red hue had the intensity of coral, glowing with warmth. The beads looped forward like a garter. Or a noose. They led the eye into the painting's low heart, twisting, coaxing you further back before finally coiling, serpentine. The transmuting coral beads were charged.

At least, this was how they seemed to Clarice—but it was often hard to predict the effect a work would have on others; would they be stirred? The edge of shock in Meldrum's silence, however, told her that he saw it. He was affected.

'You've used the paint well,' he said finally. 'You haven't just pushed it around with your brush like most students do.' He sounded troubled. 'Nice and thin. No superfluous brushstrokes.'

She lifted her face, absorbing the compliment, waiting for the verdict.

'Quite alright,' he continued slowly. 'I wonder about that red, though.'

'For the beads?'

He nodded. 'Was that exact?'

'Exact?'

'True. It seems a bit high-keyed. A bit *strong*?'

The criticism she had heard from him before was solidly dismissive, sharp, even barbed. It was odd to observe him lenient.

She spoke in a rush, without reflecting that he was probably not used to defiance: 'No, I think it's right. That's what I saw.'

He looked at her as if just roused from the solace of a thick sleep. And she gazed back, not finding it in herself to be falsely modest or evasive with this teacher she admired. They measured each other up. He was not a ladies' man, though perhaps he noticed her also as a woman.

'It's the effect I wanted.'

'That was the actual colour?' He was testing her.

'As I saw it. Yes.'

'The draughtsmanship is good,' he said carefully. 'You studied with McCubbin?'

'Yes.'

'And you took drawing classes before that?'

'As a child. There was a Miss McFarlane.'

'Ah.' He half smiled, as if acknowledging that there was always a Miss McFarlane, in some shape or form. 'And she identified your *aptitude*?'

'Yes,' she said, suddenly more vulnerable. 'But I've always drawn.'

'I see.' His intonation almost ironic, faintly entertained— not disparaging. Meldrum turned to consider her landscape.

A dim city street in fog or fine rain. This could have been a view through a mesh of eyelashes, or captured by some instrument tenderer than the eye. There were parked motors and a few people on a footpath, though they were hardly there, the human figures, just hinted at. There was an awning and a sign attached to a building, likely a theatre; these adorned with flecks of orange and yellow, electric lights. Other small lights, some the headlamps of approaching cars, were dotted spectrally through the dewy blur of an evening.

He did not speak for a while, and then he observed, 'Interesting. This is quite modern, isn't it?'

Modern, related to art, was usually a dirty word in his mouth and now it had to be coming, the reprimand.

Instead: 'You are not new to landscapes, I gather?'

'No,' she admitted—or was it a boast?

He looked at her again, seeing her as she had scarcely been seen before. Quietly, he said, 'You've rendered the tonal values sensitively.' More reluctantly, 'And overall, you're a fine colourist.'

He wanted to criticise it, rebuke her, she understood this, but he was not sure how to go about it. He seemed disarmed. It was a singular experience.

'It's modern. But I think I see what you're after, I think I do.'

Her teacher did not warn Clarice away from landscapes, back to safer indoor terrain, though she imagined he was asking himself if she might be a little mad. It was much more than she had hoped for, a victory, maybe the beginning of an awkward respect. She was incredulous and wanted to shout.

'I look forward to seeing where your work will take you,' he said. 'I mean, once your style has settled down.' And this was his way of reasserting his authority, the final sign that her paintings had shaken him.

They were not quite friends after that, but their exchanges held the suggestion of a friendship, of a stern, restrained kind. Meldrum marked the backs of his students' paintings with a grade, A, B or C. Clarice took his hard-won marks to heart, and before turning over a painting to see what she had earned, she was apprehensive. She began to receive a few As, then mostly As, and she never had a C. She had heard him declare women incapable of giving themselves completely to art, lacking a propensity for solitude. But his behaviour contradicted such unoriginal and limited beliefs. He sometimes praised Clarice over the boys and used her paintings in class as examples. He seemed now to consider her his star pupil.

3

Miss McFarlane came to the house in Casterton above the Colonial Bank once a week for a year to give Clarice and Louise a drawing lesson. Mum had met her through the church choir and formed the opinion that she would benefit from some extra income; she had only a few private students and it seemed was not very well-off. Mum also believed in the value of creative occupations for one's leisure time, in artistic accomplishments for girls and women. She was attracted to Culture, associating it with elegant grandeur and civilised pleasantness. She herself had painted a little, before Clarice's memory began, and two souvenirs of this foreign time, watercolours, graced the walls of her bedroom when her children were small. Clarice stared at these for long periods, enthralled by the watery, slightly smudged look of them. One was of crimson rhododendrons in a green vase. The other, of a single bird-of-paradise flower that floated in the air. The areas of colour were bright and gay; they gave you a happy jolt or else grated on you.

Clarice had once overheard Mum say to Henrietta, the maid, 'Clarice is a natural drawer.' Mum's soft voice even more whispery than usual, as if she were telling a secret. Proud but wary.

By the time of the lessons with Miss McFarlane, when she was ten, Clarice had seen that Mum's watercolours were only prettyish and slightly good. This hurt a bit. She still enjoyed gazing at the bird of paradise, the better of the two: it did remind her of the flower—dazzling, both flower and bird, with that stiffly birdlike attitude, watchful and distant.

'The girls are artistic,' Mum liked to tell company. 'They take after me.' A facility for creating likenesses had been identified in each of them. Clarice drew relentlessly; Louise, when bored or wanting attention. She was four years younger and babyish. Clarice had never been that babyish, she believed, and neither had the little one, Paul, who, a year younger than Louise, had more of a right to be. He rarely drew, but when he did, it was scenes from his own imagination, with a great frightening strength, objects or creatures colliding, or poised in an intense stand-off. The girls were encouraged to sketch flowers, corners of their home, or each other. The latter held little appeal; they were more inclined to draw Mum, desperately competing for her approval. It was better later in the day, if she sat reading or embroidering, her face not tight, public and symmetrical anymore but drooping, her eyes more searching and sometimes slightly pained. Usually, though, she insisted on posing dressed up, hair freshly done and wearing her expression for the mirror, half smile and half moue. You could not draw her properly like that. Louise gave up as soon as she had the mouth too large or the eyes too close, and even Clarice lost interest quickly. She was uneasy drawing Mum, wishing the mother in the picture to be beautiful, to shine with easy unconditional love. So much simpler to draw objects, houses, plants or the cat, Daffy. It had been decided that Paul would not participate in the lessons with Miss McFarlane. Perhaps he did not want to, or perhaps it was because his drawings never looked like anything you recognised, seeming to belong in dreams you would wake from afraid; their parents said he was too little, though they also occasionally described him as precocious.

Mum greeted Louise's efforts as triumphs. It was hard for Louise to sit still and concentrate; if she did so for the time it took to finish a drawing, then this was an achievement. Mum and Louise both fought against quiet, needing to be busy and to have other people around them to be cheerful. Mum said, glowing, 'Louise is very vivacious.' There were sometimes graceful details in Louise's drawings, but she ruined them by not looking carefully for long enough. Clarice's drawings were also praised, joylessly, and she turned over in her head the comment about being a natural drawer. A compliment—but not. Meaning that she did not have to try, that drawing well just came to her.

The drawing did come to her. It came because she was waiting for it; she was prepared. At times, she tried so hard that there was nothing left in her afterwards. It could be exhausting to look in that way. 'What am I going to do with you?' Mum might say, kissing her forehead at bedtime. 'My introvert. We need to bring you out of yourself a bit, don't we?' *Introvert* may have come from Father, who liked to sum people up, often ending a conversation: '. . . Well, he's an expert,' or '. . . an incompetent,' or '. . . a liar.' Drawing was being *in* herself. If you came out of yourself, where would you be?

Miss McFarlane was refreshing, like half-light, so different to other women Clarice had met. Though she was an adult, she did not give the impression of being completely grown up. Her plain dresses were worn with a straight, supple back. She was comfortingly and thrillingly serious. And she was also beautiful, actually, in a bare fashion, except for her extravagant dark-red hair that was out of a fairytale. This was restrained in a very neat bun, as if someone had angrily brushed and pulled it hard into place for her; the bun loosened over the course of an hour, fine silken tendrils making a gaol break.

The hour felt longer than an hour, slower, floaty—then it was crushingly over. Clarice was always grieving for the last lesson and starving for the next. Lesson was a funny word for it, because there were no real commands and you did what you would have chosen to do yourself. You could be 'moony'. Slowly circling the desk at which the girls sat, Miss McFarlane made suggestions if they were stuck, but these were light and did not upset. She said they would find their own way with art, if they were patient and committed. Sometimes she spoke of perspective, something Clarice thought she mostly knew—had suspected, at least, even if she had not had a word for it before or felt it needed one; the more the word was in her mind, the more complicated things got and she was likely to confuse herself and make a mess.

Miss McFarlane's hands were what Clarice adored most about her. Unless they hovered or fluttered a little, with curiosity, she kept them folded together under her breast, or placed them behind her back, one hand holding one elbow. They were careful and decided. Her long fingers had intelligence, though probably many of the things they knew, they would keep to themselves.

If the teacher was pleased with you, she did not flatter, did not gush, as Mum did; you believed her. Maybe she considered Clarice capable of more. For example, she often gave them different subjects to study. Clarice's might be a surprising branch with a bulbous bit on it like a knuckle, bark peeling off or disorienting colours, and Louise's an easy common flower. One afternoon, after settling Louise with a dainty rose, Miss McFarlane took a seashell from the big floppy bag she always had with her, and placed it before Clarice.

She worked at her drawing in a state of extreme nervous concentration. Finally, sweating, she saw that her seashell was too small on the page. Not much of a seashell. Odd and silly, as if she had scribbled. It resembled a cloud, more than anything. Her throat turned narrow and sore, her nose burning, as if she had breathed in water, swimming.

Miss McFarlane leaned over the desk. She laid her hand on the girl's shoulder; it exuded gratification. Clarice was confused, and slowly it dawned on her that this was a special message: Miss McFarlane had been ambitious for her and found her worthy. She struggled to see her seashell as the teacher might. Did the clumsy shape promise something, the way a seashell did? Make you think of something much bigger? She was not sure. But how marvellous that to fail could be a kind of success; it was entering a world with rules that were impossible to predict.

Miss McFarlane smelled as if she had eaten an orange without washing her hands afterwards. 'Very nice,' she said of Louise's fancy, hurried rose. Perhaps it too was a success, if you saw it differently.

Clarice wanted to be kind to Louise. It would not take anything away from her. 'Lovely,' she added.

Louise could tell that something important had passed between the other two. 'Show me that,' she said skittishly, and Clarice's desire to be kind hollowed.

'No.'

Louise, strong and determined, snatched her strange seashell away.

'Give Clarice her drawing.' Not exactly hard, Miss McFarlane's voice, but meaning business.

With passionate indifference, Louise crumpled the edges and left a profaning grey thumbprint before surrendering it; she had to leave her mark. The final flourish was a plaintive smile.

The best revenge was ignoring her. But it was difficult to look away from her dark hair, pink skin, and eyes that were lively when she was happy, which was most of the time. *Vivacious.*

The teacher had gone, Mum seeing her to the door and Clarice hanging back, not wanting to watch. Louise was in their bedroom, singing, freed. It was such a relief to have Louise in a different room, with space clarifying where each of them ended.

Striding to the kitchen, Mum called, 'Why don't you go and lay out your clothes with your sister?'

Some of Mum's friends and their husbands were coming for dinner, and she was propelled by the contented anxiety of all this; Father was less fond of company, but from time to time he indulged her, sulking a little. Clarice loitered in the hallway, marooned somewhere between the drawing lesson and the paler activities that lay ahead. She was trying to ignore Mum's conversation with Henrietta, but made out, 'I feel awfully sorry for her, without a family of her own. She'd be so lonely.'

'Did her husband pass away?' Henrietta asked reverently.

'No, no. A spinster, poor dear. Daffy, out of the kitchen. Scat!'

The cat loped into the hallway on three nimble legs. A rabbit trap had stolen her fourth. Daffy gave Clarice a quick look that suggested raised eyebrows, then slipped, yellow-grey eyes emptying, into the frame of mind in which human matters were irrelevant.

'But she's attractive.'

Miss McFarlane?

'Yes, isn't she? That auburn hair. Bad luck, I suppose. She never met the right one.'

'Poor thing.'

'She could still, if she keeps her wits about her. She has a neat little figure that lots would envy. But she can't wait forever.'

Miss McFarlane; not married. Clarice was shocked by Mum's superior tone, Henrietta's *Poor thing*.

Amazingly, the windows in the front room, when she went to them, framed Miss McFarlane, who was still on Henty Street, outside the bank. Rummaging in her floppy bag. Had she lost something? The teacher looked as if she were talking to herself in her own head, thinking no one was observing. There was nothing unlucky in her appearance, certainly not in her dignified hands that were perfumed from an orange. Her beauty was not on account of her hair—that was somehow the least of it—but of there being nothing *extra* to her. She was gentle and stark, like silence. Spying, Clarice was a little frightened, as you can be of silence, even though you want it.

Miss McFarlane found what she was looking for, or remembered where she had left it, and was on her way. Clarice imagined the room that she lived in: it would not be in one of Casterton's more handsome homes, such as their own above the Colonial Bank; you would probably need a morose, bossy bank-directing husband for that. A modest room in which to loiter and draw in a restful half-light, eating fruit or just lying on the floor, face turned to the carpet. Perhaps with a cat, which would play only when in the mood.

When Miss McFarlane left for New Zealand to be near an ailing relative, Clarice mourned.

4

The day Miss McFarlane was framed by the front windows, so private and contained, searching then satisfied, could it have been then that Clarice realised there were roads you might choose over marriage, roads involving art? Before she got to Meldrum's classroom, she had received several proposals or near-proposals. She had come out at eighteen, her mother cooing over the official photograph for which she had scrubbed up so well, the implication being that she could be attractive more often, if only she would try. Louise commented that she was diaphanous in it, and laughed; Louise thought Clarice considered herself above everyone else, ridiculously ethereal, or something of the sort.

The first offer came the week after the photograph was taken, from an acquaintance of the family, Jim. When they used to vacation at Beaumaris, not imagining they would one day live there, Jim, his younger sister Nellie, Louise and Clarice all played together on Sandringham Beach, as children do, by turns improvising and regimented. Little

Paul, who was slightly *different* in a way the adults, without explaining it, clearly found embarrassing and oppressive, never penetrated the games. Jim and Nellie had been judged good playmates because their father was an engineer and their mother a pious person, apparently, who kept a flawless house in Brighton. Jim was kindly and not unimaginative, with a good instinct for the arrangement of interesting driftwood or shells and a pleasant, light manner of teasing you out of a funk if you were sad.

But as can happen, he had flattened out in the process of growing older and trying to make himself into a man, and by the time he started coming to 'visit' them at Casterton, he had a hardened posture and the makings of a cocksure swagger he was developing. A shame. There was no perspective to him anymore, nothing to look back into, no vista. Finding him rather insipid, when the proposal came, she turned him down. Mum was horrified; he was going to be an engineer, following in the proud paternal footsteps, with a bright future, et cetera, and Father thought him an upright citizen—high praise.

Nothing after Jim for years, then, in the way of attention from men. That is, other than the usual games of glances— at social functions, in the street—driven by off-balance impulses. She was sometimes prey to romantic daydreams; a man's quality of gaze or gesture could set off an odd quickening of her pulse, a piquant fancy, which usually deflated quickly.

The next open expression of interest in her came from the distinguished Mr Dagdale. She and Louise had been allowed to leave home to live in St Kilda, at Elenara, a guesthouse on Fitzroy Street, so they could attend the Gallery School. For Clarice, this was all intoxicating, but Louise's interest in study was half-hearted at best and she had immediately begun to play with the idea of dropping out. Mr Dagdale was often on their tram, going to or coming from the city. Clarice quite admired the clean, unobtrusive way he inhabited the fresh or softened creases of his pinstriped suits, and the diligence in his reading of newspapers, however his attraction to her felt courteously distant. It may have been that this distance was not on his side of the line that separates two people, but on hers. He delivered his proposal in a hushed monotone, standing on Fitzroy Street, his formal figure set pleasingly against the Cricket Ground, almost silhouetted; she had no notion of his substance. The sunset was beginning. The changing light made her think of getting down to the beach. His hands looked reliable, and rose-coloured reflections moved over the lenses of his glasses, but she was distracted by the saffron cloud formation above him—vast and majestic, like some recumbent god. Though she did not mean to offend him, she was brusque in her reply. Mr Dagdale folded his newspaper carefully before he walked away. Looking back on it, she would realise that she had been cold, possibly cruel.

The next offer—or almost-offer—of marriage was a more significant matter (for Clarice, at least: she did not know what she might have meant to Mr Dagdale). Thomas was a fellow boarder at Elenara, well ensconced when the sisters arrived, having been there for some years already. It was alleged he was in his forties, and a lifelong bachelor. Certainly, he was not very outgoing but had the attitude of one observing from the sidelines, which is perhaps why Clarice found herself warmly disposed towards him.

The first time they passed on the pretty, carved staircase, he expressed an interest in the sketchbook and boards she had with her. She showed him a couple of things and he was thoughtful and appreciative; he went on to tell her that he sometimes consulted art books at the Public Library. She liked that he was enthused by art and took her seriously. He was lanky and slightly stooped, his hair very ginger, his face grave.

'Would you like to come up for a cup of tea?' he asked. This became their custom. The cups of tea were accompanied by impressive sweets, often Spanish, treacherously crumbling, enormously sugary concoctions made from pulverised nuts. He obtained them through his family's business—the importation of exotic foods and luxury items, such as the weighty bricks of soap from the south of France he once gave her—that was run by his older brother. They had lost money in the nineties, but there must have been plenty left over because there was never any evidence of Thomas doing a day's work. He tried to enlist when the war broke out but had not passed his medical; there was a problem with his hearing. After this, he abruptly changed his mind about the war, about war in general. 'I was suffering from a patriotic delirium,' he confided, suggesting that his own infirmity had saved him from unimaginable horrors. Clarice nodded, indeed unable to imagine them,

25

and said nothing. She herself had a hazy sense that nationhood should not be invoked to condone violence. Once she saw him on the banks of the Yarra, amid a group listening to what she thought was a communist speech; she did not join them, though for a moment she considered it. She planned to investigate politics, one day when she was less engrossed by the river, less troubled by how to bring it onto her board. Thomas seemed to settle into a kind of cheerful pessimism that only confirmed him as an epicurean and an aesthete.

Giving onto the Catani Gardens, where the rotunda, the palms and the pines, their tops like elongated drifting clouds, were all so elegantly outlined at dusk, Thomas's rooms were among the nicest at Elenara. They were clearly a bachelor's residence but were attractively chaotic, littered with books (Henry Lawson, Dostoyevsky, Baudelaire, Karl Marx) and gramophone records (Satie, Debussy, American jazz), biscuit tins, and invariably a saucer bearing a strainer clogged with swollen dark tea-leaves in a tannin-rich puddle. The first time she came, he insisted Clarice take a chaise longue patterned with red flowers. Impossible to imagine his angular length arranged along this piece of furniture. Keeping primly to the edge, she sat achingly straight-backed. The next time, however, resting on one elbow, she tentatively half reclined.

'Is this what psychoanalysis is like?'

'Tell me anything that comes into your head,' he said, with a wonky smile.

'Must I talk?'

'No, of course not. Have a nap, if you like. Don't mind me.'

During the following visit, she slipped off her shoes and stretched right out on the chaise longue. Early on, with Thomas, she might have been testing just a bit her ability to attract him; she was quite new to the effect she might have on a man. Would he be noticing her ankles and calves as she lay there? But soon she stopped asking herself such questions and was natural with him and rather serene in his room. She enjoyed his company, his relaxed manner. They developed a routine for saying goodbye. When she was ready to go, Clarice sat up and slowly put on her shoes. Then she stood at the window, looking out. Thomas came to stand beside her for a minute or two, close enough that their arms sometimes touched. It was companionable.

She was fond of him. If some weight had subtly shifted, their friendship would have tipped into romance or what is called romance; the possibility of it, though unacknowledged, was palpable. Clarice realised she was in danger of moulding herself to what she imagined was the shape of Thomas's desire, of playing a part, because it appeared scripted. She did hope for love: there was anticipation in her. But she resisted this, waiting for something more unequivocal and visceral.

She saw how it could have been between them, saw him make the first overture, his hand shaking lightly as it lowered over her hair, herself receiving the caress. She saw what a life with him would look like, the nights shared in bed, the two of them listening to the wind and laughing at random, minor jokes, the day's flotsam, and perhaps turning to each other eventually, comfortably affectionate. Their rooms tropical from the perpetually steaming tea-kettle, the surface of the table lingeringly sticky with sweet crumbs. A snug life. With a silly subdued merriment, she would call Thomas *T* and he call her *C*: 'What do you say to that, T?' 'I don't know, C—how about you?' She would have some time for her art and he would be proud of the results. When she returned from painting, he would hug her, saying, 'I missed you. You smell like the sea.' From their peaceful indoor complacency, she could contemplate the park across the street, and the bay lying quiet or in different stages of turmoil beyond it. There would be days of virtual silence and days with the wireless on, days of reading—Clarice reading to Thomas, loudly so that, with his faulty hearing, he would not miss anything.

But she was quiet-voiced. Would she easily grow accustomed to speaking loudly? Would he occasionally fail to hear her? This might have been a foolish fear, as naturally no one ever quite hears your thoughts; they are too multiple and slanted. She saw herself after his death, some years before her own, distraught. How distraught?

About to put the kettle on for tea one afternoon, Thomas said he was all out of matches and would duck out for a box and be back in a jiffy. Clarice offered to go, but he insisted she remain, leaving her sitting at the table before a plate of Turkish delight. Next to the sweets, a book. She opened it idly: photographs. There were naked women in the photographs, some of which were beautiful. The models' faces were fascinating—either a little dead, or stunningly unguarded yet self-possessed.

She heard Thomas return, his footsteps, and the matchbox rattling on the landing before he came in. He found her bent over the book.

'How dynamic,' she said.

'I've got the matches.' He held up the box. 'Yes, those are quite good, aren't they?'

There was a sudden strangeness between them, their bodies now a collection of angles jutting into space, where they had worn it smoothly. She closed the book and got up.

'I'll have to skip the tea today, actually. I've some things to do. Can I take one of those?'

'Of course,' he said, voice slackening. 'Please help yourself.'

She picked up a pink gelatinous cube, gingerly carrying it away between forefinger and thumb.

That night she slept poorly, and she woke very early the next day, dressing straightaway. Most mornings she managed to creep out without waking Louise, a heavy sleeper. A force, some possession or homing instinct, would tug Clarice out of bed and across the road, through the park and towards the water. There, she sat on the stone wall, stood on the sand or got as far as the end of the pier.

But that morning, though she opened the door with exaggerated delicacy, it clicked and Louise was woken. A few moments before, her sister had moaned and flung an arm out from under her quilt.

'Sorry.'

'What time is it?'

'Early. Go back to sleep.'

Louise rolled over, grunted and fumbled for the watch on her nightstand. 'Lord. You must be joking.'

Clarice put her hat on.

'You're truly insane.'

'Probably. Bye.'

'Hold your horses.'

Clarice sighed, took off her hat and stepped back into the room.

'Come here for a minute.'

She left her hat, coat and sketchbook on a chair and slowly approached Louise's bed.

'Sit down.'

She almost missed their old life at home, where at least Louise had had a variety of people to focus on. She hesitated, then sat.

'Don't go out in the cold at this godforsaken time.' Louise grinned devilishly. 'I've got a wild idea. Go back to bed. We'll have a sleep-in for once and play truant today. I'm thoroughly sick and tired of school. We'll have biscuits and tea for breakfast in our pyjamas. I've got a packet of shortbread creams stashed away. It'll be fun! We could even invite Thomas if you want. Or would it be better with just us girls? Then we'll go into town. I need a new dress. So do you, badly. We'll go to Myers. It'll be great.'

'I don't like missing classes.'

'And that's why you should. Come on. Just for this once. Don't be so boring.'

Louise was holding her arm, and Clarice felt her sister's energy, her will. Her warm morning breath, sweet and sour.

'I'm going out to draw.'

'You're so *studious*. You make me feel old.'

'We are old, for students.' No one ever guessed they were twenty-seven and twenty-three. They were both young-faced.

'Speak for yourself.' Louise leaned forward, naughty eyes flashing. 'What are you wearing?'

'What? A jumper.'

'*My* jumper.'

'Don't be ridiculous.' But it was, in fact, a little large on her, a little wrong, somehow. Louise's camel-coloured jumper. 'Oh, for heaven's sake. I obviously couldn't see what I was doing, getting dressed in the dark so the light wouldn't wake you.' Louise was having a wonderful time. 'Anyway, you must have left it on my side of the dresser. You're not going to be such a hypocrite'—maddeningly, Clarice had now started to laugh at her own hauteur—'as to refuse me the use of your clothes?' Louise 'borrowed' Clarice's clothes very often, feigning ignorance, to get under her skin. Clarice sputtered, the sort of hysterical laughter that exhausts itself only to start again. Louise kept triggering it with her high-pitched giggles that always set other people off, making trivial situations irresistibly comical. Clarice often thought Louise's states of extreme amusement forced, but just then, laughing, she thought, I'm sometimes too stiff with her. She noticed she was tired, a slight dizziness and irritation at the corners of her eyes. And Louise looked tired too, her merry eyes puffy and the skin of her cheek bearing the diagonal imprint of a rumpled pillow; Clarice had an uncharacteristic sensation of older-sisterly concern.

'Go back to sleep. You need more rest.'

'I do. I really need my ten hours.' This was not laziness, Louise claimed, but biological necessity. Maybe. People were so different from one another. Still, Louise had a way of protesting, insisting on her own special rights.

'I know you do, dear. Lie down.'

Louise lay docilely back, enjoying being mothered. If Clarice did not go quickly—she felt, without being able to explain why—she would not escape.

It was still well before sunrise when she stationed herself on St Kilda Beach and began to sketch, blind. It was crucial to her training, this struggle to create a likeness without being able to discern in the conventional way either her subject or the marks she was making on paper. Approval and rejection suspended, the movements of the charcoal in her hand were cushioned by darkness, by the sound of the waves. Art, maybe, was this honing of instinct, a process so intimate as to be almost invisible. Nothing was more real.

She started to make out what she was drawing, or thought she could. The pools of seawater strewn on the sand by the tide now held a white marmoreal light. The clouds were in infinite soft banks, the moment in loose parentheses. An insomniac dog walker passed her, but respectfully they did not disturb one another. When she had finished, she squatted to examine a huge yellow starfish, dead and light. With the toe of her shoe, she teased the unclouded perfection of a bluebottle till it trembled violently. Near the shore, the water was crystalline, the air warming and brightening; she turned and saw the first lemon hint of sun at the horizon.

She recognised Thomas's long form, hatless, coatless. He was at the end of the beach. He had followed her.

He had trespassed. She did not want a witness.

He raised his hand in an ill-defined wave and she tried to smile, but it would have been impossible for him to be sure of her expression at that distance. He had to be cold, dressed so incompletely. He was threatening the self-absorption that she needed; that time must remain pristine. Turning back to the water, she thought, dimly: understand what is happening here.

No verbal offer was made by Thomas, but his following her that morning constituted, at least in retrospect, the most eloquent proposal she ever received; and her turning away an unambiguous answer.

For years after, from time to time, Clarice saw the homely tableau they would have made: him reading in an armchair, her reclining on the chaise longue as she gazed out the window, through the palm trees, to the water. She liked to think she would have known how to accept his goodness and repay it. They promised to write, of course, when she left Elenara to live at Beaumaris with her parents, but that was just to be polite.

5

It was an excellent, indispensable thing, the mobile easel, a veritable studio on wheels, practical and liberating for those who worked *en plein air*. She was one of the first of Meldrum's students to adopt it; many of them followed her example, seeing the convenience and freedom it afforded.

Father would not allow her a studio in the house, but a painting trolley he could hardly say no to. Especially as she went ahead and constructed one herself. As it turned out, the trolley was better than a conventional studio, because it had you continually out in the elements. She had never fathomed nor respected the notion of 'poor' weather. Poor? Where most people saw something dismal, Clarice revelled in the quiet sumptuosity, or moody turbulence of greys. In general, grey was so little appreciated—but what of the curiously luminescent bark of gum trees, the ocean turned to mercury by the moon, the simple reflective wonder of a wet road? The lowered light of overcast skies, rain or fog was good for painting, making it easier to distinguish tonal differences. Full bright sun did not show you their delicate divergences, but rendered everything stark and hard-edged, so you were not quite sure in what order you were receiving nature's impressions.

Aside from going proudly into bad weather, the trolley was a superior studio, because—obviously, but not trivially—it was not stationary. It worked thus. The body of the cart held your materials (boards, brushes, paints and so on), while extending vertically up from this was the mast of the easel. The handle was comfortable to use, both for drawing the trolley along when you were on the move, and then for shifting the easel back and forth once, a spot decided on, you were in the thick of work. A lot of going back and forth between the observation point and the subject was another of Meldrum's teachings that she liked and made her own. The trolley very nicely enabled you to bring the board right up alongside the subject, so they could be compared from the observation point. An active style of work that to a non-initiate must seem a puzzling little dance.

She savoured it, the dynamism, and all things considered, her trolley served her better than a studio, spoiling her with air and space.

The house in Beaumaris was bought after Father's retirement—prompted by his delicate nerves—from the Colonial Bank. Louise married after a brief courtship and gave birth to a baby boy. Overjoyed to see her younger daughter so finely established, Mum grew visibly worried when Clarice, unmarried and at home, passed the age of thirty. She never came at the subject directly, but often enthused over the beauty of Louise's little Ron and the ample satisfactions of motherhood. She imagined, she said, that Clarice must be looking forward to having her own family, and once asked about the existence of a male friend. Never having learned to confide in her mother, Clarice fairly effortlessly avoided any invitation to do so.

Louise and Mum did confide in one another, however, and between them they cooked up the scheme of bringing together Clarice and Stanley, a close friend of Louise's Ted. Clarice had met Stanley at Louise's engagement party and at the wedding, and Louise had reported dryly that he thought Clarice a beauty. Clarice had nothing against him. He seemed affable, but somehow her mind slid right over him; she had trouble remembering what he looked like.

Then he came to the house with Louise and Ted, the three of them dropping by, artificially casual, just after Clarice and her parents had finished a stodgy Sunday lunch.

Finding herself alone with Stanley in the dining room and feeling obliged to say something, Clarice inquired after his work. He was a furniture maker. This aroused her interest, because she had respect for manual work and, thinking of building herself a painting cart, she wanted advice. She explained how the cart had to function and, after some puzzlement on his side, a rather intense conversation ensued. By the end of it, Clarice was holding a sheet of paper on which Stanley had drawn a diagram of her cart in its stages of assemblage and written her a list of instructions. She had thanked him warmly. Excited by the idea of her cart, she had not stopped to consider that the enthusiasm she was seeing in Stanley, his livening face and pell-mell sentences, might have been the result of something other than professional interest.

'I could make it for you,' he said. 'Otherwise. I'd be happy to. It'd be no bother. None at all.'

His cheeks were flushed and there was a patina of triumph in his eyes. She had encouraged him; he felt they had arrived at a new intimacy.

This unfortunate impression was confirmed by Mum a few days later, over breakfast, after Father had gone out for his stroll. 'Stanley wants to start a family, you know. He's tired of being a single man. He told Ted.'

'Oh?'

'Yes. The furniture business is doing very well and now he finally has time to think about his personal life.'

'That's good, I suppose.' Clarice poured them each a second cup of tea that would have a bitter aftertaste.

'I'm not at my best this morning.'

'No? In what way?'

'A bit tired. Exhausted, really. It must be my heart.' Mum suffered from a weak heart, as her mother had. It was believed that Clarice did too, although she herself considered this an improbable piece of family lore: she had never felt remotely weak of heart. Mum smiled gently. 'It's affecting me more these days. Dr Broadbent told me it would, as I got older. Of course, I haven't been the same since your brother.'

It was unusual for Mum to talk of Paul, who had ended his own life ten years previously in the asylum at Kew. After the initial shock, his name had very rarely been spoken in the house—even less than during his two years in the 'hospital'. There had always been a great silence around Paul, as if it could have been capable of cocooning the unexplainably odd kernel of him. Since he had passed on, Mum mentioned her heart more often, this was true, and perhaps did seem more fragile.

'You should take it easy today, then. Rest yourself.'

'He's a nice young man, Stanley. We've invited him over this weekend. For afternoon tea.'

Clarice was looking through the window at the lovely blue-purple mess of wisteria draping the shed at the end of the garden, which housed her paintings.

'And so you and he can have a bit of a chat,' Mum continued. 'Get to know one another. He admires you. It'll be quite informal. Louise and family will be there.'

Clarice scraped at the burnt corner of her toast.

'Is that alright with you, love?'

She did not make a scene. 'It sounds like everything has been arranged.' Despite her anger, which she struggled to repress, she perversely did not refuse the afternoon tea. Perhaps to spite the meddlers: because they would be pleased with themselves, and then disappointed. They would learn it was a mistake to try to direct her behaviour.

This was, of course, misguided, and the repercussions of her passive outrage were entirely awful. The suitor invited to tea. All of them gathered, stiff and ludicrous, in the drawing room, the air pervaded by the family's approval of him as a fine prospect. In their tension, she thought they resembled hopefuls assembled for an audition on which a lot is riding. She pitied them; pitied herself. They drank their tea with frequent small sips from the special china, a blue and white fantasy of pastoral England wrapping itself around the cups, spreading over the saucers, like an extravagant rash.

Stanley's eyes, boyish and self-congratulatory, not even a little melancholy or doubting, kept going to the photograph of Clarice at her coming out, positioned strategically on a cabinet by Mum. The photograph, some twelve years old now, showed her from behind, glancing sideways. A romantic profile genteelly embellished with a lace collar, pearl earring, softly piled hair. So feminine. Clarice attempted to ignore it.

She choked down weak tea on a chair beside her mother, feeling horribly exposed, regressed to childhood—which was appropriate, as that whole civilised disaster was the result of an invisible tantrum. She had had to dress up, sucking in her breath to get the top hooks into the eyes of her best skirt; when it moved with her steps, the black silk made a slight whispery music she liked, though the firm waistband alerted her to the nervous action of her ribs.

Stanley's expression showed a steady trust in his own wishes, in a convincing story he was telling himself. She esteemed this, to a certain extent. He saw them—he and Clarice—shoulder to shoulder aboard the great ship of matrimony. They were ageing good-naturedly as the mysterious shoreline of her deep self receded. There was a fatalist momentum to it and she would not succumb. She noted a new resistance in herself; living with her parents again was bringing out in her something disobedient and wiry.

He and Mum had been carefully discussing the conscription debate, but the platitudes had gone as far as they could be taken and there was a pause. Louise and Ted looked at one another, as if listening for the baby, who was sleeping in a cot in the sewing room. Deep quiet. Father profited from the lapse in the pleasantries to make an exit; he was probably suffering from his fatigued nerves. And now Mum, with amused indulgence, said, 'I should leave you young people to talk.' She stood and moved towards the door, and stopped. 'Was that the little one? Louise? Do you want to look in on him? Or should I?'

'I didn't hear anything,' Louise replied cheekily. 'Ted, did you?' Louise and Mum doted on one another, but there could be a teasing friction between them. Louise had permission to be mischievous.

Mum laughed. 'I'm sure I heard something.'

Ted was on his feet, impatient. 'Come on, dear.'

Louise raised her eyebrows. 'I don't know why, but I've come over all sleepy.' She yawned flirtatiously, then, with becoming lethargy, reluctantly stood, linked her arm through Ted's, and off they sauntered after Mum.

Silence submerged the room. Their gazes entangled, trying for innocence.

'The tea is very weak,' Clarice commented, enormously regretting this charade, this elaborate hash.

'Oh, no,' Stanley assured her. He was a decent man, who did not deserve to be in such a situation. 'It's fine.'

'I like my tea milky,' she went inanely on, 'but it has to be strong. Well brewed. I don't like it weak.'

He coughed. 'I'm not a strong tea man.'

To prevent him from saying anything embarrassing, she blurted, 'The cart turned out fantastically. I made it without any problems.'

'You did it yourself?'

'I told you I would.'

'Yes.' He evidently had not expected she would be capable of it. 'That's . . . impressive.' It was hard to tell if he found the achievement admirable or off-putting.

'No cuts or splinters.'

'I think it's wonderful that you paint. I play the violin a little myself. Pretty terribly, but I can pull off a few tunes, more or less. Though the violin is unforgiving.'

'So is painting.' Clarice was becoming irritated, all the more so for having brought this torturous conversation on herself, and on poor Stanley.

'Yes, of course. Irish music is my favourite. There's a lot to be said for having something creative to do in your spare time.'

A nervy clack of china against china; she had lowered her cup to the saucer more forcefully than intended. 'I don't paint in my spare time. When I'm not painting, *that* is my spare time.'

'Oh, I see.'

'I make time to paint,' she said quickly. 'It's my most important activity.'

'I see what you're getting at.'

He was gathering himself now to say what he wanted to say and it made her queasy. 'Let's go out,' she said, springing up from her chair.

'Out?'

'Into the garden.'

'For . . . a walk?'

'I'll show you the cart. And maybe a painting.'

'Right. Fine.'

Outside, the wind was sweet and ticklish with wattle, the day bending towards late-afternoon gold. Her breathing deepened and her spine lengthened. With what might have come across as haughtiness, she led him to the end of the garden. She would have liked to be kinder to him, but she would have had to let down the necessary defences.

'This is a good, big yard,' he said, glancing at her. 'It's getting chilly.'

'Yes, it's bracing.' Reaching the shed, she turned to him. 'The cold focuses me.'

She kept the shed locked because she could not stand the idea of her father poking censoriously around in there. She let her parents see her art as little as possible and only when prepared. There had been an occasion, when she ran into the house with a painting she had just then completed, to present it to them. A view of the Bay Road, a Model-T Ford from behind, a curious shadow thrown by a gum. Clarice was inebriated with what had happened: she had directed her full attention at a landscape, that landscape had returned the favour by looking right back at her—with the same intensity—and she had tried to capture the shared look in paint.

Her parents adjusted their glasses, drew breath.

'Ah. Well,' Mum said, after a moment, labouring at tact.

There was a smart-alecky light in Father's face. 'The sky is a funny colour,' he contributed.

Later, Clarice would see that attempt at the Bay Road as painfully imperfect, laughably flawed. The perspective awkward. The shadow not right.

But their failure to find important what had seemed somehow holy to her came on Clarice like a physical attack. Beside the point, that their opinion may have been correct. It was subtle, dressed in mildness, and they were no doubt ignorant of it; nonetheless, she suffered it, in the moment, as an attack. She half laughed and, before understanding the action, flung the painting across the room. It hit the wall, caught on the back of a chair. Fell, finally, to the floor, face down. General stupefaction, as if she had just confessed to an outlandish crime. Clarice, the quiet introvert, had done this loud, appallingly emotional thing. No one spoke or made a move to retrieve the painting. She turned and left.

Returning some hours after, humiliated and now humbled, she found the painting on the top step of the verandah. Reproach? Apology? Who had left it there? They had shown her it was hideous, her own presumptuousness; Father was not mistaken—the sky was a fancifully ardent, hysterical turquoise. She picked it up with the heartbroken futility she might have felt handling the corpse of a young animal. The paint was a little smudged, but the board was intact. She wished it had cracked.

'Terrific,' Stanley said, inspecting the cart. He frowned thoughtfully, running his hand over the surface, suggesting that he himself might have done something differently.

He was a craftsman, after all, and building things with wood was his trade; however, she did not much care for the insinuation of his superior manly expertise. While he lingered over it, she considered which painting to show. One to demonstrate how foreign she was to him—irrevocably. Providing it was not to her parents, she had lately discovered that she was able to show her work with less discomfort than before. Or rather, it was still exquisitely difficult and wounding when the viewer was indifferent or critical—and hazardously delightful otherwise. But she could take a step back, as it were, spiritually slip away. An enormous relief, because paintings had to be offered.

It was a small tool shed, too narrow for a studio, though she might have tried to use it as one were it not, alongside her paintings, also packed with the sundry boxes that overflow from a family home.

'Very nice,' he said. 'I recognised her immediately.' From over her shoulder, he had peeked at a portrait of Louise: a painting from before Clarice trusted herself with reality—Louise looking self-effacing, without her sparkle of mischief, less seductive than she was.

'I'll show you something else.'

'Not only beautiful, but talented,' he murmured, behind her.

She ignored this gesture at flirtation, going through a stack close to the door, relaxing in the odour of oil paint.

Something unpretty. Something people found murky and bleak. This.

Scraggly, minimal brushstrokes. Nothing but the essential. A rocky brown cliff. The sky and the sea dissolving into dark mist. These were the bones of a landscape, shining indistinctly like bones, a low twilight throb.

'Here.'

His smile faltered.

6

'How did it go?'

'A good morning,' she said to Herb—a permanent fixture on the beach those past weeks. A sort of camaraderie had developed between them such that sparse words were plenty. She had met him in Meldrum's classroom, a broadhanded rubicund man with considerable intuition and a careless grin. He liked to quote Thoreau, saying intently, *to live deep and suck out all the marrow of life*. He was going to France soon, and before doing so had determined to suck the marrow from the Australian landscape. He was living in the caravan-studio he had had custom-made. Most of the time, he kept it parked by Half Moon Bay and there had been some complaints, but he resisted moving on. Herb had achieved a gypsy existence in the service of art and it made him buoyant, as if he might become airborne at any moment, rise up and float away.

He glanced at her work, nodded. Then looked again, for a little longer. He only ever approached her when it was clear she had finished. Herb himself was splattered cheerily with blues and reds, a wandering palette.

'Tired?' he asked.

'Not now. You?'

'Fit as a fiddle. Tea?'

'Oh, yes.'

He made for the caravan. As Clarice methodically packed up her kit, she noticed a man on his morning walk. The Doctor. They had never been introduced or said hello; local gossip had taught her his profession. She saw the Doctor most days, usually in the evening, knowing his silhouette and slow, sure-footed steps almost as if he were a feature of the landscape.

She joined Herb by the caravan. She took her tea from him and nursed it in her cramped hands. The blessed first cup of tea. Leaning forward on camping chairs, they studied the day: perfect, nearly smug, it might have been congratulating itself on inventing the idea of day.

'I won't be able to stay much longer,' he said eventually. 'They want me away from the beaches.'

'They're mad. What harm are you doing?' Her voice was rusty, not yet self-conscious. 'Still bent on France?' Everyone seemed to lust after France.

A beguiled smile. He was lighting up with exoticism, with the immortal feeling that comes from closing in on a dream. Perhaps she would miss his laconic companionship, when he went. They understood one another and his enthusiasm was a tonic; she laughed.

He seized her empty cup. 'Coming in for a swim?'

'I am.'

He let her change in the caravan. It was innocent between them. He might have liked it to be otherwise, but he appeared to appreciate that it was the generous distance in their friendship that made it. Inside, his caravan was somehow roomy, holding a vocation and the few, rough-hewn pieces of an itinerant life's jigsaw puzzle. Herb had driven through South Australia in this, crossing deserts. The incestuous jostling together of art and day-to-day existence, the whiff of grand emancipation, pleased her immensely. As she undressed, her eyes travelled obliquely over her now remembered, renewed body; she was well coordinated, unhesitating.

They stood in their bathing suits with just their ankles submerged, feet taking root in the liquid sand. It thrilled them that they had spied on the beginning of the day, had participated in it; they felt young, in the best way: bold. The water was an amazingly cold reward.

The sea gave itself entirely. It did not hold back, having no modesty or reason for restraint. It surrendered because it never lost anything. The water's embrace was soothing and alarming; she was never sure out here which had the upper hand in her, happiness or crazed fear. It was the world in raw form, the swimmer constantly on the edge of the precipice, kicking to stave off drowning, deceptively weightless.

TWO

The First Blow

7

Clarice saw him for the first time on a Tuesday promising rain.

She was early for class and, on her way there, she had paused to admire Princes Bridge. Her notion of what was interesting—aesthetically pleasing or beautiful, you might call it—was large and flexible. She was not concerned with grandeur or decoration, and she ruled nothing out. Clarice loved her city well, comprehensively; all its plain, enticing fragments. A length of half-empty road, a long wistful shadow stretched out over it. An arrangement of telegraph poles. Some were offended by change, but she thought it a pity to see progress as the enemy of beauty—because then, you were left only with nostalgia, having turned your back on so much that deserved your attention. An infinite-seeming number of small and indispensable views asked to be looked at, demanded it, and proceeded to etch themselves onto her awareness. It was usually after she had finished a board when she realised that a painted view suggested something beyond itself: the substratum of an emotion, the air that a story might pass through. On that Tuesday of imminent rain, she saw Princes Bridge. A slice of it: the solidity of cast iron resting on bluestone bulwarks, and the steady current of traffic this carried. The palm trees in the foreground, in some way endearing, self-consciously adolescent. The little boats on the mirroring water beneath and above, a maternal, impersonal sky. She thought she would do a quick sketch or two and a colour study to fix it in her memory.

But she was soon busy with a panel, squeezing obliging worms of paint onto the palette, adding a little of this and some of that and working it together with rhythmic, religious rigour till her colours came towards what she saw, like a tentative meeting of strangers who have recognised something in each other.

The trance released her when she had done what she could do. She enjoyed it this way, painting in one fell swoop. *A premier coup*: at the first blow. A storm of painting quickly arriving and departing—a transient frenzy. The finished painting was different to the picture she had held in her mind before beginning. It was never, of course, that perfect. You did what you were able or needed to do at that moment, tried to accept it, to be unafraid. She was developing.

She entered the studio quietly. Holding the panel with care, she was mindful of the impressionable baby-softness of its wet surface. She pegged it to the wall at the back of the room for drying. She had not quite exited the painting yet; sometimes she lingered within a just-completed work, reluctant to go.

One of the young men, Henry, came to see.

He laughed sharply, in spite of himself. Then he hurried over to where the other students were sitting in a loose but attentive group. Ada came to stand beside her, staring at the fresh paint. She had heard it said that the girl was an imitator of her style, but this did not bother Clarice. If some people occasionally did not know to which of them to attribute a work, Clarice herself did not see any particular resemblance between their paintings. Meldrum could always tell the difference.

She became aware that the men were snickering, while at the back of the disorderly group, slightly apart, she noticed someone she had never before set eyes on. He was leaning against the wall, not participating in the laughter. He was tall and his face was tanned.

'We're not making fun of you,' said Henry, battling to be sober but breaking into mirth again. The tall man glanced at the floor, as though offended. 'It's that we were discussing it, when you came in—the very same bridge.'

He did not mean anything bad, Henry. He was one of several boys who passed the role of joker around; he was not fashioned for seriousness. Mostly nobody paid Clarice too much attention, except when Meldrum mentioned her technique. Then their mouths might twitch into slight smiles, which could have meant scepticism. Still, by and large, she appreciated the others because they cared for art; this somehow unified them all. But she kept to herself.

She was out of the painting now and looked levelly at Henry, which made him ill at ease.

The tall man's eyes touched her as she said, 'What were you saying when I came in? You can let me in on the joke.'

Like most of the class, Henry was perhaps ten years her junior. He was immature, though it was not his age. He made a stunted, comic gesture.

'That Princes Bridge is an eyesore. With those horrid palms.'

They laughed because she had chosen to paint what they deemed unworthy of paint, the refuse of blemished modern Melbourne. It was always newly startling to discover that her subjects were considered unsightly or irrelevant.

The tall man was still not laughing and it appeared to her that he had quiet, uncommon ideas of his own.

Clarice did not want to explain to Henry what she had seen: the ingenuous trees, their tops like unmanaged morning hair, and the rhythm of their vertical offerings to the horizontal bridge, which was itself a homage to the horizon. The optimism of it, the fallible humanness. She reddened. Clarice's and Henry's ideas of beauty were incompatible.

Her smile was diluted. 'It took my fancy,' she said.

Someone giggled.

'Oh, leave her alone,' Henry mumbled, but burst into strident laughter, the others joining him.

Clarice laughed for a moment too, then noticed a spot of paint on her cardigan. Ultramarine. It would not come out.

'You're unimaginative,' said the tall man to those who had laughed.

It was a clever insult to direct at artists, a dire pronouncement, and they were shamed. He had taken revenge for her.

As though he were offering her an arm for support. She had a sense of accepting the arm and standing up straighter beside him. The room had been pacified, now harbouring softly cloudy light. His authority animated it, each detail of the space made significant by its proximity to him. He was closer to her in age, she thought, than to the younger ones.

Meldrum made his usual decisive entrance, on a mission. They moved to their places, metamorphosing into mute students, acolytes.

Meldrum stopped by the tall man, addressing him respectfully, 'Arthur.' It was the first time she heard his name in anyone's mouth.

The two men shook hands; as Arthur gave his right hand, she saw the wedding band on his left. A ring—that cool, conclusive statement of ownership. Of fate decided.

And she heard the other name. 'It's good to see you here,' Meldrum continued. 'How's Bella?'

The question constricted her chest, somehow more than the ring. She felt bitterness for that bouncy bubble of a word, *Bella*. It was at this point that she weighed her desire, so overblown it must be the blossoming of a longing that had always been in her, growing; simultaneously, she understood how it could be thwarted.

After class, a bunch of them decided to walk to the station together. Henry sidled over to Clarice, by way of an apology for before, and asked if she would go with them. She was rubbing futilely at the paint stain on her cardigan. She had overheard that Arthur would be among the group. They were all taken with the novelty of him.

'I'll tag along,' she said. 'Thanks.'

She dawdled, packing up. He was behind her.

She turned and . . . yes. He—Arthur—was at the back of the room, leaning towards the panel she had hung to dry. He was studying it.

She thought he blushed as she came near.

'You have quite an eye,' he said.

8

The low sky thickened, like a white sauce reducing in a pan. Clarice and Arthur walked behind the others. Wisps of conversation reached them, a mention of Freud. Someone was doggedly analysing last night's dream.

'You have an umbrella,' Arthur said. 'Do you have far to go at the other end?'

'No, not far.' She heard her voice, feeble and intent on lightness. 'Anyway, I don't mind rain.'

'I'm the same myself. People are always complaining about the weather. I like any weather.'

She nodded. It was necessary, safer, to be sparing with words. As if they were spies, every element of an exchange and the interplay between the elements had to be evaluated. She had not felt this before with a man. He seemed to be trying to adjust to the rhythm of her stride. She listened to the city, people packing up shop, heading home or for a drink, rushing to catch trams or trains, pausing at doors that were entrances or exits, depending on the direction of one's intention.

Up ahead, Henry was evoking a dream in which he was a king. He expounded on the kingly trappings, fine clothing, jewels and several buxom wives. It did not have the feel of a true dream. An inaudible, evidently bawdy detail provoked guffaws. The party atmosphere was Arthur's doing. It was his confidence, his casual splendour. They were not brave enough yet to talk freely to him, but he agitated them.

'I wouldn't know how to tell a dream,' Clarice offered. 'To put words to it.'

'No. Probably wiser not to.'

She watched a man catch a hat the wind had pulled off his very smooth, bald head.

'We have a daughter,' Arthur added, after a while.

'Oh. And you enjoy painting?'

'I don't know if enjoy is the word. It's new for me.'

She had begun to tremble earlier at the studio, when she sensed him behind her and then saw him looking avidly at her board. But the trembling was moving to her knees, spreading through her abdomen and chest, her hands and even the bones of her face; the breath in her was distressed. Though she could not have imagined it, she saw now that she had been waiting for this, for something elemental to take command of her body. Was this love?

'I live with my parents,' she said. 'I sort of look after them.'

They had been facing straight ahead, but—briefly—he glanced sideways at her. She wondered whether her eyes were greener or browner at that moment, if it mattered, what kind of a woman he glimpsed.

9

A month had passed since his arrival in the studio. Already, though they were only cautiously friends, she knew much about him, collecting facts. He was a shy painter. Painting appeared to be the one area in which he was shy. He was unhurried, loose in himself, most of the time. His stance related easily to the ground beneath him. He walked strongly, seeming to expect a steady flow of good luck. He observed the moving shapes of the sky in the way of country people. He took control of a room without trying. He was a relaxed talker and a teller of stories, loving to entertain a group and quite humorous when the mood took him. Not talking was not a problem for him, however, as it can be for those whose talk is smooth. Silence flattered him like a high-class suit, a generously positioned lamp.

'Out there', as he sometimes said, he was a lawyer and you imagined him in this role as trenchant and formidable, always winning his cases. In fact, it turned out he was rather renowned, his name often in the newspapers. Whereas in the quieter world of painting, he was an unknown and a neo-phyte, feeling his way. It caught Clarice's attention: he had reduced himself to this. He chose to be unsure, to proceed unarmed, surrendering to the experiment. He was humbled and perhaps a little afraid with a paintbrush, which he held solemnly and also self-mockingly, as if it were a mast bare of flag and he could represent only his own dreamed country. Arthur the man, keen to be a schoolboy again in Meldrum's classroom. He was both a natural and a self-trained watcher, the good kind; he had sensitivity and maybe a scholar's humility.

And she had seen his wife. Bella. In a spotted, black-belted dress. Not the child, thankfully. But the Mrs in her spotted dress, the wifely existence of whom could not be denied. His other half—which was not right, as he was so frighteningly whole on his own. Whole, yet questing, his gaze bruising what it passed over.

Arthur was a whetstone keeping her sharp, over-alert, per-verting her nights so they became a wakeful, sickly, queerly self-satisfied torture. The nights could be difficult. But they ended with a morning-to-be like this one, the fragrant world latent in the reddish dark and the cart in her hand roll-ing single-mindedly on its wheels towards the sea. When Clarice got to Black Rock, the waves were gentle, nocturnal yet, almost soundless. And she was besotted. Besotted with the sea and besotted with Arthur Blackburn.

A visual imagination can be a scourge and, with her

mind's eye, she saw scenes she would rather not have been privy to: Bella's hair being brushed by lamplight, the ripe swelling of her belly with his child, their rapturous intimacy. It seemed unfair that a woman should have a name meaning beautiful, as if she had the monopoly on beauty. Clarice had not found Bella stunningly attractive, not even particularly comely, however she doubted her own perception. There had to be rare loveliness in a woman with such a lucky name and destiny. Perhaps it lay in a detail not immediately obvious. The sinuous volumes of her thighs. Her warm, private smell. Or—painful to consider—some quality of her heart.

Clarice was wretched from wrong, incessant thinking and under its spell. She was often cruel to herself in those days, vindictive, punishing herself in little, secret ways, pinching the flesh of her own arm or biting her tongue that threatened to speak. She was brutally exacting with her art, hating most of her paintings, once they were complete. But she was still too self-indulgent and undisciplined to rein in her truant mind. She was really only tranquil when properly in a painting; that was her respite.

She settled into a spot on the beach, separating her feet the right distance, stretching her toes inside her shoes. Mercifully, extraneous thoughts were dispersing, dropping away. The dawn began and she lifted the cart's lid, entering the usual strange meditation. She emptied so she could fill, or was it feel—differently, calmly? She rubbed her hands together, getting the blood flowing. Looking. Impressions travelled towards her like wave fronts through a kind of ether. Her brush in a loose grip, she was part of a design larger than her own, deeply scientific or inscrutably holy.

Afterwards, slightly cold, she stood in her bathing suit close to the sea. When pictures of Arthur returned to surround her, a dense fog, she jogged into the water.

Swimming, she followed for a while the cool, majestic progress of an ocean liner, vaguely curious about the intrigues and inner lives of its passengers. The mindless gliding of gulls held her attention longer, as did her astonishment at how a lone body, hers, could disturb and alter a wave, so subtly. Time was soft and the universe fecund. She discovered, putting her chin to it, a strand of seaweed on her shoulder, verdant and fishily alive. It stayed where it was, amiably claiming her. And there was more of the plant floating about, like her own marine hair. Those were her long, luxuriant tresses: she had intermingled with the watery element. She was anaesthetised.

But here was Arthur again, bringing back the new ignited Clarice. Coming in, chilled and shaking, she found Herb on the beach. He waved and she approached. He was sitting drinking tea and smoking, pleased with himself, carefree, irreverent. 'I've been round at Sandringham,' he said. 'What a day for it. I drew the fishermen with their nets. Magical thing. You'll have a cup? I've got a fresh pot brewing.'

The morning was getting on and there was not long left, the minutes shrinking quickly. 'Lovely,' she said.

He looked her up and down. 'You'd better get some clothes on.'

In the caravan, her damp nakedness was preternaturally white. She dressed, and forced her hand through her tangled hair. There was a sketchbook on the cot. She thought of the airiness of fishing nets, which Herb—with that weightless quality of his—would know how to convey, but she did not open it. He sometimes asked for her opinion on something and she was always reluctant, thinking it better not to look at a friend's work that way; she might be hard on it, as she could be on her own. But she had seen a few of his paintings, and liked the pioneer hunger they had in them. Where would this take him? Back in the expanding light, she was shivery, jerky.

'I must be coming down with something.' She watched the swirl of milk on the surface of her tea, a white spiral staircase slowly undoing itself.

They sat for a few minutes, the sun hot but not quite easing her chill.

As if apprehending the drift of her thoughts, Herb said, 'You should get yourself a boyfriend. It would do you good.' He glanced away. 'I hear on the grapevine that someone has rather taken to you.'

She had jumped a little in her chair, unmasked. She laughed—a husky, staccato attempt at subterfuge. She saw that it had been unsuccessful. 'Oh, really? He has a wife. Didn't you know?'

'I hadn't noticed.' Herb slurped his tea. 'The little problem of marriage. Would it be a problem, though?'

She had a twitch of irritation. He imagined that the lives of others should be as easy and light as his own. They were all masters of their own fate; surely they all enjoyed the luxury of improvisation. And he did not consider how different it was for a woman. Conspicuously, she ignored him.

To appease her, he said, 'Thought I'd drive over to St Kilda in a bit. I don't suppose you want to come along . . . we'll have our own art camp?'

The day had grown yellower and broader.

'Duty calls,' she replied, somewhat tetchily. 'They'll be wanting their breakfast.'

'And what will *you* be wanting?'

'I won't be studying with Meldrum much longer,' Clarice found herself saying, after a moment. 'Not much longer at all.' It had been in her thoughts, had been coming on, but she had not announced the decision until now; her path sounded surer than it felt. This was not to do with Arthur. She must try working as an independent artist. Herb was watching her, curious. Perhaps he was impressed. She got up. 'I'm off. Thanks for the tea.'

Her teeth were chattering on the way back. Not even the forced pace of the walking warmed her, yet she was hot-cheeked and, unusually, found herself craving domestic work, that well of dullness; she wanted to drown in it. Could the others believe that Arthur liked her? Liked her, not platonically? Could this be a common view? When she stopped going to Meldrum's classes, she would no longer have to see him, not in the flesh, anyway. Would it be easier?

At home, she hurried to put her cart away in the shed and set the awful painting to dry, then headed for the kitchen for something to occupy herself with. She stood savagely rigid in the centre of the room. The first thing her eyes caught on was a cookbook lying on the counter. She seized and aggressively opened it at random.

'*Cakes*,' she read aloud.

'Clarice, dear?' Her mother's light singsong from the front room.

'Yes, Mum. I'll be in shortly. I'm getting breakfast on.' In a lower voice, she continued, "*The success of a cake will depend entirely on the baking, and on constant attention. Be sure to test the heat of your oven.*" She repeated these lines several times over, one hand gripping the book, the other on her hip to keep it quiet.

Once the trembling arrived in her, it did not leave. It dwelled there. Sometimes it was slight, hardly noticeable, but not so she could forget it; other times, it was as if she were just then emerging dripping from the bay on untrustworthy legs. It was always there, thrumming along with other pulses that threaded invisibly through life and were its vital energy. Her shaking affected things around her in such a way that nothing was left slack and certain ideas were given a breathtaking impetus. Though it was an impetus that, for a very long while, would have nowhere to go.

10

During the year since she had ceased to study with Meldrum, she had continued to drop into his studio from time to time to show him her work, and he invited her to exhibit several pieces in his first Group Exhibition. It was a serious, Spartan affair, the paintings listed in the catalogue without titles, black frames all around. The look of that long wall of the Athenaeum Hall, dense with art. Forbidding. Pure! Five of her paintings were there, an honour.

The hanging had captivated her. What next to what? What above what? And beneath? The arrangement of a show was not straightforward; it was a question of design, rhythm. She took a long time over the hanging of her works. She agonised, her back burning. She dithered till she was—almost—content. Paintings grouped together could be mirrors. The right placement would angle them towards one another so that each melted into and deepened the others, giving a feeling, soft, powerful, of amplified space.

At the opening, she was unspeakably proud of her

temerity. She—yes, *she*, Clarice—was exhibiting. This was part of being an artist; you had to do this. She was elated and terrified. It was a rowdy crowd of intellectuals, art people, eccentric and original, or more conventionally fashionable, and others who belonged to who-knew-what passions, fixations. The talk flowed in excited eddies and she did not follow its circles. Her position in relation to any group was always at its edge or beyond. Arthur was there, though he had nothing in the show; painting for little more than a year, he had not felt ready. It was months since her last glimpse of him at the studio. He was like a painfully handsome groom, in a black suit and extremely white shirt that gave his skin the appearance of milk tinged with coffee. He looked as though he had not expected to find himself there, yet he was not out of place. She had an urge to stand near him, but did not give in to it. They did not speak or meet one another's eyes. People were attracted to him; he was always in a binding conversation.

Ada, on the other side of the room, was a little pale, her face serious and disbelieving. Was she quaking too? Clarice's eyes kept returning to the places on the wall where her own paintings hung, severely edged in black. Would she remember anything of that night, other than clamorous voices, a brightly coloured, slippery surface? She tried to focus on some of the details in all that fuss.

As if to help with this, Ada arrived beside her on the arm of a statuesque personage swathed in velvet and lace. 'Let me introduce you to Mrs Hamlin,' she said, reassuringly.

The lady's hair was golden, thick, complexly vertical,

like some fantastical plumage. 'What a delight to meet you. I'm so taken by your paintings, which are absolutely exquisite. Delicate! I don't have words for them. You must be a highly, an unusually sensitive person. I can tell.' Her manner as velvety and intense as her dress. 'I'm a bit of a patron of the arts.' She beamed an enormously satisfied smile, finding everything delectable. 'This is one of the things I'm most proud of. You see, my husband, Mr Hamlin, has been successful as a jeweller and I've had advantages. I try to use them well. Some years back, I fought for our suffrage. I used my influence in little ways.' Clarice's own achievements, on the wall, now seemed rather questionable. 'But returning to the topic of art, I'm a great admirer of Mr Meldrum. And I'd heard of you, but this is the first time I've had the pleasure of observing your art first-hand.'

'Clarice is a unique talent,' Ada said. 'It's almost unnatural—everyone is in awe of her, even if they don't let on.' She laughed modestly. 'She intimidates us.'

Seeing Clarice's face, Mrs Hamlin said, 'Surely you're not surprised. After all, you're the artist most represented here tonight, after Mr Meldrum.'

She desired and dreaded this singling out. She knew, of course, from his words and acts, especially from his mannerisms, that Meldrum appreciated her work. The choice of so many of her paintings for the exhibition had only really been a minor shock—more a confirmation. But she had not been sure of the others' opinions. They had laughed at her Princes Bridge; she was taken aback by the idea that she might intimidate them.

'I'd be honoured to buy one or two of your canvases,' Mrs Hamlin went on, 'but we'll talk about that later.'

'There's so much confidence in her paintings,' suggested Ada, with an odd formality, as if too timid to direct this at Clarice. 'I wish I had her confidence.'

Confidence seemed a strange word, when she was suffering this stage fright. 'Painting, you can be yourself,' Clarice said, recalling that Ada was thought to copy her. 'You try to be yourself. You don't always manage it.' She raced on: 'At these things, who are you? I never know. I'm very awkward.' Rather pathetically, she blushed; you were not supposed to admit to social unease.

Mrs Hamlin took her hand for a moment and pressed it. The contact was calmly firm, anchoring. Clarice tried to smile. The lady holding her hand was long, solid, queenly, magnificently rounded in the shoulders, and the rest of her, too, was covered generously with flesh. Mrs Hamlin said, 'You'll have to get used to intimidating people. Men will be alarmed, because you can do such things and you're beautiful, also, which will confuse them. One rarely sees a fair skin as radiant as yours. That's another sort of beauty I have an eye for. I'm a beautician. For my own pleasure—my husband sees it as a hobby, an interest rather than a profession, but I take it quite seriously. Manicures and pedicures are my area of expertise. I've been told that my own feet are a work of art.' Was this intimate information proffered to balance Clarice's declaration of discomfort? 'And not just by my good husband.'

Ada wore a faint smile, perhaps picturing those feet, as

Clarice was. She saw them oversized, on a statue, in marble, gleaming. Her brain was absorbing Mrs Hamlin, becoming permeated by her; people could flood you. Had Clarice been inclined to do such work, this woman would have made an intriguing subject for a nude—what would you find beneath that velvet and gloss, her solidity and great capacity for enthusiasm?

'Your work would be interesting,' she said, not really able to imagine it but not insincere.

'It is,' Mrs Hamlin affirmed. 'And I think I feel so close to artists because my work is also about beauty and nature, natural beauty. We have a lot in common. I have many artist friends, we get on so well. We see the world in a similar way. I love being around you.'

Clarice laughed gauchely. And she noticed, when Ada said, 'Your dress is a lovely colour,' how good the girl was with people, light-handed.

'Lavender,' Mrs Hamlin said. 'It's special, isn't it? And feel that.'

Clarice, too, automatically put out her hand to stroke the dress; the texture was quite hypnotic. Mrs Hamlin was now studying Ada, wanting to compliment in return. But they were so different. Mrs Hamlin large and full; Ada petite and slight, lightly freckled nose, plain dark dress, brown hair neither really fair nor dark, all quietly pleasant. She had an air of knowing herself to be unassuming, forgettable. And this made her a thin presence, somehow, the thinness accentuated by her gentle way with people—which was probably rather tragic.

'You're charming,' Mrs Hamlin eventually told her, kindly, and the girl bowed her head.

Clarice was suddenly very grateful to be in the company of these gracious women, to have merged, however briefly, with the evening's stagey talk. It took her mind off Arthur, the too-handsome bridegroom, her paintings on the wall, her frightened vanity, the grandiosity and shocking immodesty of it all. It let her share her happiness.

As usual, Father was done with *The Age* before Clarice and her mother were up; he must not have seen the review, as he had not made any comment. He did not read the cultural sections, as a rule. Meldrum had told the class that it would be coming, and the anticipation had kept her awake all night. Now it was Mum's turn with the paper; she was perusing the front page, peeling and cutting into small pieces an apple, which she slowly chewed and ate. She had an upset stomach and had wanted nothing more, not even tea. Clarice was anxious that Mum would see it.

'It'll only make me more nervous if you come,' she had said, when Mum offered to go to the opening. This was true. 'It might be better if you don't. And it would tire you.' Her mother had agreed. Had she really wanted to go or only felt obliged?

After the apple, Mum lingered over a glass of water, the paper forgotten. A curious object, densely black on its whiteness, soft and thin, while so authoritative. If Clarice had taken it to her room, it would only have drawn attention. But she had to look now. 'Are you finished with that?'

'What's that? Oh, do you want this?'

Opening the paper nonchalantly, Clarice stalked it. There, there was her name. In print. In a real newspaper. With a deathly calm face and frozen lips that wanted to mouth the words, she read what a Mr Chesterfield had written.

Oh. And charged through to the climax: 'And the lady has no right to obfuscate her subjects so tenaciously with mawkish veils of fog. The result is altogether dreary, and, I regret to say it, entirely without the lyricism in which we seek solace in art.' He had noted, subtly venomous, that her paintings were 'sub-manner' and unfinished, as if this were something to be feared, abhorred. She had hoped but not expected that they would like her work; however, she had not quite foreseen this. She was not the only one from the exhibition to be condemned. In fact, condemnation was the general response, really—not even Meldrum was spared. But still, this felt appallingly personal.

Having read her first review, she folded the paper neatly, stood and left the room, abruptly reminded of Mr Dagdale, the day she had rejected him, his folding of a newspaper and stunned, grave retreat.

Like being cleaved through the middle, she thought, gutted—because maybe quickly describing the sensation would numb it. In the hallway, she paused and placed a hand on each wall. So the critics did not have much time for the 'Meldrumites'; they were 'mud-slingers,' with their dull, mucky palette. But why could art not show nature, as it was, without embellishment or forced emphasis? Trust nature to be beautiful, on its own terms? Reaching her bedroom and finally closing the door, she found herself on her knees. She might have to be sick.

Some time later, Mum knocked on the door and opened it.

'Clarice? The telephone for you. What? What are you doing down there?'

'Thinking.' The worst was passed, the nausea gone. She had not heard the phone.

Mum was waiting.

'I was feeling off,' Clarice tried to explain.

'Could it have been the porridge?' Mum asked carefully. Did she know about the review? If she did, neither of them was going to mention it.

'Porridge does make me a bit queasy, sometimes.'

'Porridge is like that.' Her mother was probably relieved not to be faced with any more substantial vulnerability. They were cautious together, when it came to anything private.

'You might have this same upset that I have. Do you think you should see Dr Broadbent?'

'I'm a lot better now.' She was. Almost strong. Standing, she was only slightly unsteady. 'I'll get the phone.'

'The porridge? Do you think?' Mum seemed concerned. 'Something we had that your father didn't, because Daddy is fine.'

Mum was the only one who called him Daddy; he presented Clarice with the phone, looking indeed as if his health were beyond question, indomitable. He disapproved of the telephone for anything other than emergencies: it was for communication, not conversation. When he himself was forced to make a call, he took notes beforehand, the process efficient, exact. 'It's Ada Anderson,' he said questioningly.

'Thank you,' she said, taking it and turning her back on him.

'I'm calling to commiserate. Are you alright?' Ada's voice was cheerfully melancholy. She had not been mentioned in the review.

'Thanks,' she said. 'I'm alright.'

'It's just bitterness. Bitterness against Meldrum. He's the target. They won't forgive him for spurning the Gallery School. For having pluck and going his own way. You're his best student, so they're taking it out on you. They haven't even *looked* at what you've done. They don't want to see it. You can't take this to heart.'

'Everyone got a hard time of it,' Clarice said. The hurt mixing with fury now, and she could be angry for Meldrum, for all of them. 'The only serious art is big bright sentimental potboilers. Apparently. You can't show the smaller view, the real colours of the Australian landscape. That's unacceptable. Not heroic enough, I suppose.' She was nearly pleased to have provoked them, and sorry that Ada had been left out of it. 'How are you, Ada?' She should invite Ada over for tea one of these days.

The girl rushed by the question, embarrassed or unaccustomed to having others consider her feelings. 'Your art is important, Clarice. But it's easier for them to discount you as a woman. Mrs Hamlin is right—it confuses them. You'll have to get used to it.' Could she? Clarice asked herself.

Would they always have such a view of her? 'You don't paint as a Lady Painter should.'

Father passed the doorway, checking his watch. Still angry but also increasingly pleased with herself, she said, 'No, I don't.'

11

The week after the opening, on an excessively luminous, unseasonably hot day, Mrs Hamlin threw them a party in the garden of her stately home in South Yarra. Arthur, thoroughly one of them by then, did the honours and took a photograph of the artists uproariously arrayed on the lawn. Under the sun, a tablecloth, a handkerchief, a woman's high-collared shirt, a rather incongruous goat were all celestial; Clarice was dazzled by so many white forms, containers of light. She felt the dizzying suspension that precedes an Event and it cost her a considerable effort to control her trembling. She gritted her teeth.

The picture taken, wine was drunk amid growing amusement. She toasted with the others, to art for art's sake, to life, to everyone's health, to goats, to the entire animal kingdom. She was not used to drinking; one of the few outward signs of Father's Low Anglicanism was his scathing view of alcohol; equating it with swift and total moral decline, he did not allow it in the house. The music was persuasive, divine coils of Debussy unspooling from a gramophone through an open window. This was followed by other music that was new to her—faintly but persistently troubling, liquid; it released something in her. The crimson wine, too, spawned obscure impulses and left dark perfect rings on the table-cloth. She drank two or maybe three whole glasses to soften the idea of Mum at home: she had appeared a little glum as Clarice prepared to leave; her stomach was not quite back to normal and perhaps she would have preferred her daughter at home, for company. Those glasses of wine must have induced the migraine, though the beating of her head took some time to distinguish itself from merriment. It was a marvellously bohemian afternoon, pain holding her skull like a large, insistent hand.

Meldrum, dapper as usual in a dinner suit, held court on the lawn. The company seemed by turns a circus troupe under the direction of their ringmaster and the devotees of a sage. He was indulgent, that day, a benevolent patriarch. It made her consider the rumours of his playful side, a penchant for climbing trees; she tried to visualise him in a tree. Hard to combine such a picture with the sharper edges of his thinking, but you never knew. The sky was blue glory.

The throbbing of her brain became more commanding, something tightening in her or unravelling, and an impromptu party melody sprang up. It was a gentleman she did not know, playing jigs on a fiddle that worried the goat. Why did they keep a goat? Its milk must have gone into one of Mrs Hamlin's beauty treatments. Later, Arthur was telling a story about a drunken novice's complicated attempt to shear a sheep. Everyone was in stitches, and Clarice's belly hurt as she watched his hands elaborating the absurd tale.

When Bella came to stand beside him, his eyes fled up to the clear sky.

A scent of perfume was inescapable, sugary and heavy with roses, as was the more calming smell of cut grass. The entire afternoon was like the children's game where one spins around and around, as fast as possible, keeps spinning, although a collapse is coming and the degree of its severity steadily worsening. It was funny how eager one was to abandon orientation and balance for speed and its risks; the freedom of lost control was intoxicating, hence one's fateful inclination for it.

'Clarice, are you feeling well?' the hostess asked.

Was she wincing from the headache or smiling strangely? The brooch that held Mrs Hamlin's dress in place seemed an improbable insect, the gaudy fruit of an hallucination.

'I think I have a migraine. But what a delightful party!'

'Would you like to lie down inside for a while? The guest room is made up. A little rest?'

Clarice would sooner not have separated herself from the rare entertainment, but she had begun to screw up her eyes in the imperious sunshine. Mrs Hamlin saw this mix of reluctance and discomfort, and took Clarice by the arm. She was led inside. The hostess's ardour for artists might have contained some possessive impulse; nonetheless, she was warm and admirably colourful.

'Sorry for the trouble. I don't usually drink. That's probably it.'

'Oh, a little drink won't hurt you. It'll be the heat. But don't worry, my dear. A lie down will do you a world of good.'

The richly appointed house was a dim, soft blur.

'Thank you so much,' Clarice said, more than once. 'I'm really so sorry for the bother.'

'Don't be silly.' Mrs Hamlin helped to ease off her shoes and get her settled on a bed. 'It's a madhouse out there,' she said happily, going for a damp washcloth and a glass of water.

Clarice took the pins out of her hair. Shortly after, already in the dark of her eyelids, she felt the washcloth come down hesitantly on her forehead. 'That beastly Chesterfield person,' Mrs Hamlin said, nearly whispering. 'Plain cruel. I hope you didn't let it get to you. They just vent their grievances, while pretending to be civil. And quite enjoy themselves. Discrediting the lot of you like that. But Mr Meldrum and you bore the brunt, I'm afraid.' She was now patting Clarice's hair. 'Especially you, because your paintings are hard to put your finger on. They're atmospheric, your paintings,' she offered shyly. 'Haunting.' She seemed to wait for a response and, when it did not come, added, 'I myself was so maddened by the injustice, and depressed, after I read it, that I cancelled my appointments, went back to bed and stayed there all day.'

'Thank you,' Clarice told her. She was now also a touch drunk on sympathy and sensitivity, this *understanding*, which reached her gently through the layer of pain. 'I'm over it.' She smiled, then opened her eyes. 'Almost. You're so kind.'

Mrs Hamlin smiled back and Clarice closed her eyes again and heard, in a murmur, 'You're lovely. Truly heavenly skin. It gives off its own light.' In a voice lowered further still: 'You could make a man very happy.' Did this hold any particular reference? 'Stay as long as you like.'

A short sleep carried away much of the pain or made it into something thicker but airier. Clarice noted this when she was startled awake. She listened. Raised voices, childlike in their pleasure, the fiddle. She wriggled up so that she was leaning against the end of the bed.

In the dresser mirror, she considered what Mrs Hamlin thought of as good looks. A very pale complexion, not undignified features, perhaps—but ravenous eyes, somehow exaggerated, and what was that mark at the corner of her mouth? She leaned forward to inspect a stain, blackish, maroon, as she massaged the nape of her neck with one hand. She was boiling.

And there he was, finally.

When he had closed the door, he entered the mirror in profile; he was facing her. Arthur exhaled raggedly.

'I didn't mean to scare you. Sorry.' He appeared winded. 'I couldn't find you. Mrs Hamlin said you weren't feeling well.'

'It's just,' she said. 'It was just. A little . . .'

He gave a slight nod, and it was his turn, now, to notice the picture they made in the mirror and hers to look at him.

Becoming aware, perhaps, of her disordered state and his standing over it, he sat down on the side of the bed, with his back to her.

'Are you any better?' He was different to when they were in company together. 'Do you need anything? Can I get you anything?'

'I'm alright,' she said, grappling with the dissonance of waking; it sounded like a lie.

He twisted to look at her. It was a difficult position to sustain. He looked away, and back. He put a finger to his lips and brought it to the colouration at the corner of her mouth.

'I don't know where that came from,' she said. 'I was just wondering what it was.'

'The wine,' he replied, looking perturbed. 'We don't see enough of you.'

His hand did not withdraw and so she turned her head to kiss it. This was not audacity. She had no choice in the matter. Taking his hand, as if it were a surprising new invention, she drew his mouth to the place his finger had encountered. It happened fast.

The surprise of the kiss. An assertive flavour of tobacco. After that, the taste of his own exotic mouth and of his desire for her. It was her first real kiss and she would not forget it. The unveiling. Smooth heat. Blind tunnelling from one interior world to another.

They were very quiet. Arthur held her hands, her shoulders, her waist; her head drumming gently, she too wanted to hold him fast. Her clothing turned oppressive, mysteriously intricate, as they tried to free her from it. At the same time, she was trying to free herself from a memory. The memory of something unreally disturbing, such as a detail from a bad dream that pesters you after waking.

It had happened a few hours earlier, before the party got going: Arthur had not yet lifted a dark cloth and, momentarily beheaded, peered through a camera's objective at artists standing to be photographed; a migraine had not yet led her to this room where he had found her. She had arrived too punctually and been invited to sit in the drawing room, awaiting the arrival of the more appropriately tardy guests, while Mrs Hamlin directed some task in the kitchen. Self-consciously alone, Clarice gazed through a window at the brightness exploding outside.

She had thought herself alone. Bella sat down opposite her, holding a precariously full glass of punch.

'Ooh,' breathed Bella, with amusement and perhaps a little nervousness. 'I almost spilled it!'

They had been briefly introduced on the occasion when Bella had worn her spotted dress. Now her dress was moss green and well cut, her purse matching. The weave of the dress was fine; it would be soft under exploratory fingers. Bella's posture somehow gave her the status of wife. Though again, Clarice was surprised not to find the woman's appearance more striking. The body before her was ordinary, disconcertingly unexceptional. In her mind, she always saw a goddess.

'Oh, hello,' she said, battling to meet Bella's eyes—a flat, uniform hazel.

'Isn't this a remarkable house?' Arthur's wife had a way of speaking that was both modest and resilient.

Where was he? In the next room? Outside under the heavy sun? A malaise was moving through Clarice's viscera. 'Isn't it? I gather Mrs Hamlin has sensational toe-nails.' Before this sentence was entirely out of her mouth, she saw it for the gossipy misfit that it was. She floundered. 'They're her pride.'

'Ah?' Bella crossed her legs. 'Her toenails?'

'Yes. She's a beautician, did you know?'

'Oh, I see. I knew she was a supporter of the arts, a staunch one.'

'That too,' Clarice confirmed eagerly. 'Actually, I don't know her very well, but she seems like a magnificent person.'

'She must be.'

Clarice touched her hair with the sudden suspicion it was untidy.

'And you're a fine painter, from what I hear,' Bella said. 'I understand Mr Meldrum holds you in high regard. That he speaks of you as the model student. My husband's impressed with you, too.' A resourceful smile.

On the end table beside Clarice's chair was a silver figurine of a fluid naked woman whose open arms held the glass globe of a lamp, supposed to represent the moon, no doubt, or the earth's sphere—some great plenitude.

'He's generous. People generally find my paintings too vague and formless for their tastes,' she said lightly.

'Really?'

'Yes. And a little depressing. Plain. Ugly.'

'Ugly?'

'They think I paint disagreeable things, anything—a street corner with a telegraph pole on it. Things like that. I will paint almost anything. It's true. A critic said, *The lady has no right . . .*' She had put on a starchy, stuffy voice, making a joke of it.

The woman grunted an amiably dismissive laugh. 'Excellent. Go on!'

'No, it's really quite boring.'

'It's brave of you to incur the wrath of conservatives.' She appeared to enjoy this phrase, but turned serious. 'Brave of you to follow Mr Meldrum. Arthur says he's a true original who sees through the smoke and mirrors and speaks his mind. That's why the art world, the old guard, is so suspicious of him, and of course it rubs off on you students. People can be very limited in their thinking. But it's wonderful you stick by him.'

'It's well over a year since I was his student,' Clarice interjected contrarily. She was weak and needed to assert herself. She continued, rather pretentiously, though without intending it: 'I really don't see myself as anyone's follower. My style is my own. I can't blame anyone else for it.'

'Well, it takes nerve,' Bella persevered, 'spunk might be the word, to be outside the main current.' She had turned her head slightly, as if searching for something out of the corner of her eye. 'It wouldn't be easy.'

'No.' Clarice was closed-off, peevish. She could not help it. 'Guess not.' She should have filled the silence that followed with an explanation and perhaps a polite question.

But it was Bella who had to speak, taking it on herself to imagine a question; she was drawing the conversation into her terrain. 'I'm very happy to be a mother,' she affirmed. 'That's not easy either.' She sipped delicately, philosophically from her punch. Then sipped again with greater determination, as though just remembering how full the glass was. Indeed, it was a miracle that none had spilled—she must have unusually steady hands. 'I suppose nothing worthwhile is easy,' Bella finished, with a tranquil face. There was not a thing more to say.

Clarice was left with the unfortunate sense that she might have liked Bella, who appeared to possess some invisible but redoubtable strength. Or if not liked at least admired her, as one admires a neat, airtight idea. And yet some hours after, without thinking twice, here she was kissing the woman's husband on his forbidden, inviting mouth.

12

In the wake of the confrontation, Father was stationed behind a newspaper in the drawing room by the droning wireless, Mum inert on her bed with her silky blue foulard shading her eyes, and Clarice in the kitchen, rapt.

Her morning's work on Beaumaris Road had been pesky but seductive, nature looking newly lustrous, baroque, somehow, in its beauty: so hard to dismantle and portray with any simplicity. She had far yet to go with her art; she knew this. But some days, she was an absolute beginner again. Returning home in a flurry, she had opened the gate and pulled her cart over the slight resistance into the yard; she was a manic Sisyphus, always lugging her burden uphill.

Father intercepted her near the verandah. He had been making his rounds. She thought this compulsive reconnoitring of his territory was a sign of restless discontent; he called it exercise. She detested being accosted as she was coming in from work—she was emotionally disjointed.

'Well,' he said. 'Let's see what you've done.' And this

was worse than usual. He wanted to see what she had been up to.

She hesitated, then tried for a very light tone, which was sometimes useful: 'Oh, it's nothing much.' On the contrary, what she had done that day was imperfect, probably failed but important and so private in its failure. 'I'd rather not.' Her coat was damp from a fine rain that had fallen an hour or two before.

'No, no. Come on, then. Let's see the *art*.'

His mistrust of it was blatant. He could not accept that she had rejected the marriage proposals in favour of spinsterhood and this freakish occupation. He might have been less alarmed to have an artist for a daughter were she less public about the whole thing and if it did not involve so much gallivanting about. Her hands on the handle of the cart, she observed his uneasiness. She moved away eventually, but first lifted the lid of the cart and propped up her delicate creation; she did not want him touching it.

The painting was a shadowy wash of silver-grey. In the background, tree trunks rose to their dissolving grey-green tops, like slender nudes reaching languidly up through the mist. At the right-hand edge, a telegraph pole was the straight, taut affirmation—the ballast—meant to keep the scene's spectral tremble from coming undone.

The strange heart of it: a car approaching, headlights casting thin yellowish beams of light onto a lushly rain-wet road that was marbled and curved like a river or some funhouse mirror.

Disquieting, really. Far from mawkish, surely. But too

KRISTEL THORNELL

shadowy? Too evanescent? Anyway, this was the painting for now; with drying, time, a different mood, it might change. New failings might be revealed. Something that had seemed beautiful as it was being made might flatten out into banality, or the humdrum could turn beguiling, unexpectedly valuable.

Her father inserted himself between Clarice and the cart, effacing it. His heavily lined face appeared sculpted. If his eyes had been a little less certain, he would have been handsome. From the old photographs, you could see why Mum had been taken with him. He had always been arresting; and pride and inflexibility seem more excusable in youth, temporary postures that might be abandoned in the next moment—an outburst of laughter sweeping them away, perhaps, and all the grim composure gone.

She looked away from the dramatic, intransigent face to the shed at the end of the garden where she was impatient to hide her cart away. The chickens were restive, their complaints repetitive, absent. She could not watch him assessing it.

He cleared his throat and leaned closer to the painting, making something lurch inside her. She would have liked to say, You are too close.

They existed in different spheres, yet he affected her. Father very naturally released an aura of power that put fear into her, mixed with a murky shame. However, he was not always astringent. He had his inoffensive moments and could even be congenial, allowing peace to flower in their house and refraining from disturbing it. But he knew how to be frightening; he was talented at disregarding the viewpoint of others, at making Judgements.

'Hmm,' he uttered, a cold declaration.

There was no poetry in him. This was their tragedy—hers, Louise's (though *she* had escaped the house), perhaps even his, but Mum's especially; because Mum was a romantic confined to a life with a man who—at least to all appearances—had a blank in place of dreams: a hollow where you would hope for inventiveness, maybe, or compassion. He stuck to the pragmatic, scrupulously denying himself astonishment. It was as if he refused to leave the close air of a man-sized box, a kind of premature coffin he bore around with him. It was difficult to tell what kept him alive. His certainties, she supposed. He was her father.

'Isn't it a bit dreary?' he pronounced at last. 'They all look similar to me, I'm afraid. But I'm no artist.'

He could evenly make a comment like this that condensed itself into something so hard that she carried it away from the encounter with her, a stone in her shoe, hobbling away and limping for the rest of the day. He upset her, sometimes. But the effect could be more ambiguous, as though, leaning forward, he had simply breathed onto the glass of her mind; his breath's milky imprint lingering, not fading or only ever so slowly, so she was obliged to peer through it at the world. His presence had become more wearing since his retirement and the move to Beaumaris. Perhaps it was having too much time on his hands or those nerves that had him tightly wound. In fact, Father did not often come near her, but he gave the opposite impression, even when they kept carefully to far ends of the house. They had a way of circling one another. And although the circle was wide, she sensed him as she would a dance partner.

'You were a dreamy child,' he noted, stepping back. 'Often gloomy.'

Her mouth pursed, she reclaimed her painting and began to drag the cart away, tossing over her shoulder, 'How astute of you to notice.'

'What was that?'

'Toast—for breakfast?'

But she could not be sad or irritable. It would have been at odds with the metamorphosis that had covered everything in a lambent sheen of new life. She fluttered.

At lunch, Clarice and Father—without even talking to one another—were somehow sparring again. He presided at the head of the table with his almost-handsome face, Mum a subtler force beside him. There was leftover lamb stew with bread and butter and an unremarkable salad. Clarice had planned and unfortunately announced a steak and kidney pie, which she had set about preparing with determination. It had burnt. A terrible waste, but she was too high-strung with pleasure to concentrate. Anyway, kitchen work was against her nature, which was simultaneously too scattered and too focused for it. So the pie had been ruined, the charred disaster quietly disposed of, and it was leftovers again. Father's suspicion of her ineptitude had been further confirmed. The kitchen smelled acridly, regretfully of smoke.

The plan was that Mum would raise the topic, and she got to it with a skilfully detached air towards the end of their hasty meal, over the peaches and cream.

In a gentle susurration, she announced, 'Clarice is going out for the evening.'

A soft voice is not always as defenceless as it seems; Mum had the trick of it. Her disposition could be fragile, but she was clever. She would not let Father dominate her and at times she swayed him or even put her foot down. As her health weakened, she became more spirited and he appeared to have less protection from her; this made Clarice think that he must love her, in his way.

He looked up, spoon in mid-air, a little cream on his startled upper lip.

'Where?'

'To visit Ada Anderson. From Mr Meldrum's school. You spoke with her on the phone, remember? Ada's father will drive Clarice home.'

She was sorry to have lied to Mum, but had seen no alternative. Mum cared for her; it was just that her attention tended to roam. Louise's absence had brought them closer. They still did not really talk, though lately there had been increasing warmth between them. Since the vain attempt at matchmaking, her mother was perhaps less opposed to Clarice's spinsterhood. If she remained baffled by the conundrum of a daughter who shunned matrimony and measured time by how long it would be till she could next be off painting, it seemed she was not, finally, entirely disapproving.

Clarice shovelled peaches into her mouth. She remembered to breathe. Father savoured an idea of himself as decisive and strict. This could be subverted or it could be quite a bother; right then, Clarice feared it. Raising his empty spoon pointedly, like an instrument of discipline, he made his counter-attack: 'Clarice is always out.'

'Nonsense,' Mum contradicted him. 'She almost never goes out . . .'

His spoon twitched.

'. . . socially,' concluded Mum.

An onerous silence as he registered Mum's coup. Such an interchange was the closest they came to a fight. Under the table, Clarice found Mum's hand and squeezed it. After a moment, the squeeze was faintly returned.

Father glanced at Clarice, at Mum, then lowered his accusing but overpowered spoon.

'She has to have a change of air.' Mum got up from the table, having given this last word, and retreated to her bedroom, where she closed herself inside an exhausted silence.

More and more, Mum resembled her voice at its most peaceful and most canny. She was becoming softer—not soft-brained but gentler in the mind, somehow, and physically, too, she was softening, her cheeks growing pillowy, her bones less obvious; there was something nebulous about her. She relied heavily on Clarice, but was in conflict with herself over this, not wanting her offspring for a servant. She may have come to realise that her daughter had needs beyond the walls of their house.

Clarice stood up breathlessly and began ferrying dishes from the table to the kitchen. Father pushed back his chair and rose, then ambled out, showing that this small defeat did not trouble his status as lord of the manor.

A moment later, when she heard the wireless he would use to mesmerise himself into submission, she slumped over the sink. In just a few hours, she would see Arthur. Her heart clenched around her excitement, like a jealous fist on a prize. Tenderness for Mum seeped through her, for the softening creature lying utterly quiet in her room; she almost wanted to go in and curl up with her so together they could slip into a lavishly upholstered sleep.

13

She appreciated that he abstained from small talk, though this left them wobbly, rather naked. A stormy feeling to the atmosphere. He wore a navy jacket and the mystery that perhaps must surround a new lover, before you have filled many of the blanks in your knowledge of him. On Collins Street, electric light spilled in glamorous waterfalls from high windows, the night a jolly, frantic spectacle. Clarice's heart beat fast. She was festive with trepidation, hoping her good hat made her sophisticated and incognito.

They needed frivolity, so he took her to the De Luxe. The thick red carpet in the picture theatre promised a rich oblivion. They sat close, naturally; she sensed the heat of his leg. It seemed to take a long time for the picture to start. Tiny bubbles from her orange drink fizzed on her nose. She turned to study the wall to her left, which was decorated with trompe l'oeil windows. The nearest framed a landscape, a steep-sided mountain, a body of water in the foreground. She wondered if he noticed her knees shaking.

The distant ceiling darkened into a simulated night; the two of them were lost in a palatial cave.

But they were not alone. They were surrounded, and their fellow spectators would assume them man and wife, or lovers. She imagined the weight of the arm he would not drape around her; someone they knew might have seen them. It was partly this awareness that had them laughing so hard with the rest of the audience at the first reel, once it began. A little too hard—a laughter that had a scared silence at its heart and ached.

There was no time to go anywhere afterwards; the hours together had been stolen time. Like a fine chocolate slipping down the throat almost before you could taste it, the treat was ending. She had been so happy, anticipating their evening, but now felt unwell and guilty.

They did not hold hands in the street, even as the crowd thinned around them. She saw his fingers stir, fall loose. The quicker it was over the better, but Arthur lingered near the van.

There was a homeless fellow on a bench close by, whom she would have preferred not to look at. He had a pink sore on his forehead. The worst was that he was reading a newspaper, or pretending to—surely there was not enough light to see by—and falling asleep over it. He would ruin his eyes. When he dozed off, the pages of the paper spilled onto the footpath, a mess. He slid down onto his knees beside the road to gather them up, the poor devil; he had a stunned look as he did this. She could not watch any longer.

She snapped, 'I wish you'd just drop me back.'

Arthur took out his keys, startled, and would not meet

her eye. He opened the door for her and she scrambled in, as if by removing herself from the view of those in the street she might erase herself. The van reeked of smoking and art: tobacco fustiness, oil paint, turpentine and linseed oil. She breathed that air greedily. His studio. This was his vehicle for escape; it could take him where he wanted to go, away— and also take him home to Bella. He had both more and less freedom than Clarice did.

She imagined stealing the van, herself in the driver's seat. Waiting a little, over the moon with her theft. And then, off, accelerating, without a backwards thought. Mr Freud's notions of women's envy regarding the male member did not convince her, but she knew herself to be horribly envious of men's vans, these wonderful means of evasion.

The chill city, then the suburbs went by beyond her immobile reflected face. Their laughter of an hour earlier seemed unreal and they avoided mention of the picture altogether. She was weary but completely awake, as she sometimes was when there was no energy left in her and she had to dig for something to replace it. She kept herself turned away from him. Her eyes were smarting. She was too aware, of everything; this night, it would have been better to see less.

Two streets from the house, in the parked van, she hung her head.

'Sorry,' she said. 'I can't stop thinking of that poor fellow with the newspaper.'

He touched her neck beneath her chignon—it was still so new for him to touch her—but she stayed rigid. It was strange that two weeks before they had undressed each other and lain down on Mrs Hamlin's guest bed, a party within earshot. She could not be calm.

He sighed. 'Don't think about anything.' He shifted closer. 'Don't think.'

She thought of Collins Street, a classy illusion. It was cold in the van. Around it, the darkness was complete.

'You have to get back.' Then, with an injured meanness, she added, 'You must get back.'

'Don't be like that. At least let me see you go in. I'll drive slowly by the house. Please. I want to see your lamp go on. Please be happy. We had fun tonight, didn't we?' She suspected he was ashamed.

She nodded.

They had to be little children for it to seem alright, or play the hedonists with no regard for consequences. But this was not Paris or New York. What if they lost their memories following an accident that left them otherwise intact? Their pasts would be quite gone, allowing them to advance through a translucent air with unknotted stomachs and no expectations guiding their steps, no routines identifying them, no one *noticing*—nothing hindering their limbs or hearts at all. In this vision, there was no harm in warming themselves by passion's fire, in taking a measure of joy.

'Do you mind if I smoke?' Arthur had his hands on the wheel now and was gazing straight ahead.

She shook her head, wondering whether physical love's highest moment had to feel like an undoing, had to shame, maim. Could it not instead be a sort of honesty? Could the joining not in some way endure?

Before he had lit his cigarette, she saw in her mind's eye a cloud of smoke leaving his lips, blue-grey and changeable, diffusing quickly—the smoke whose odour would cling to her dress as the memory of one passed on clung to a mourner.

'I'm painting tomorrow.'

He was resigned. 'Of course you are.'

She turned to him slightly, and it appeared to her then that desire could not be obstructed or dodged. It was a catchy song that kept forcing its way back into your head. It was forgotten, banished, but here was the foot tapping again. The throat humming. She turned further, laying her hand on his arm and following it down till she got to his hand that sent heat into her. He handled the cigarette nimbly, his lips expelling the drugging smoke as if knowing themselves watched, real smoke now produced by real fire.

14

The storm that had been dreaming itself finally crossed the line into being and woke her in the early hours, wind worrying the loose slate shingles. It was cool and too early to go out, so she stayed in her spinster's bed with her head tangled in the previous night. Her thinking revolved endlessly on tracks as futile as those of a compulsively circling dog. She lay there until the bedsprings creaked in her parents' room.

The day that followed was bleakly prosaic around the hiatus of painting. She arrived at the Beaumaris shore a little before dawn, pulling and then wrestling her cart. She sensed disorder.

The foretaste of light, before the sun was up, showed her what the wind had got up to during the night. A door had been ripped off a bathing box and another box thrown clear across the beach, where it would eventually be claimed by the tide. She gauged the altered geometry, the gap in the line of bathing boxes. She had sometimes found Herb here and she measured also the space created by his departure.

The artist driven out. Artists were a different breed, and of course what was different was misunderstood and almost always feared.

Sunrise seemed to come reluctantly and she felt it form and take hold of her as she fumbled with her kit in the damp, muddled time just before dawn—the darkness that was occasionally in her tingeing everything with its dark hue. The wind off the water was sharp. She fixed her focusing point, pulled her hat down lower and separated her feet further, bracing.

But then the hours of reprieve, absence, dwelling nowhere and occupying each particle of what she saw. Work. The other place.

There was a problem, early on, a blockage. She had rushed. Rushing, she distracted herself by thinking about composition. She caught herself doing it, wasting mental energy, shackled to the named world. She was not seeing but naming—bathing box, water, sky—and in this way holding on to things, stuck in their net.

She was on her own, studying under no teacher and sometimes, if this felt odd, she was able to summon Meldrum. That morning, she heard him bidding her to simplify, simplify, to forget her awareness of things.

She closed her eyes, trying to relinquish it.

Then gazed anew, cleanly at the view she was portraying and yes, found herself in the space of pure ocular sensation. She raised her palette and brush. Only the visual miracle of nature existed. Where last night she had climbed out of Arthur's van, releasing that particular dream, now she gripped the hand of reality. She would not let go. She painted, speaking only the universal language of depiction, a scientist of the visible world—or perhaps, though this could never be said to Meldrum, some class of medium or mystic. The fine movements of her brush sewed her own fibres firmly to life.

In the end, when she laid her brush down and finally invited words and the things they named back like reprimanded children from the other room, Clarice thought she had the proof of her diligence. She had transcribed the visible, some of it at least; there was some truth here. She showed the seascape to its reflection in the mirror she had made. There.

The bathing box at the shoreline and everything suspended, nestled within a smoky haze. The brownish-olive cliff. A suggestion of the curve of the next bay. The water, nearly flat: pink, grey, white, blue. One sensed that the ocean was not senseless but a sentient, musing thing. The bathing box's torn door was iron red. Across the expanse of water, beyond early morning's cloudy drift, a softness of coastline.

She hankered for salt on her skin, but it was not a day for swimming; it was cold and chaotic and her body too unrested. She packed up and took the path between shaggy, dispassionate gums, wattle and tea-trees. Concentration and clarity left her, now it was over, and she was gone to the dogs. The cart was even more unwieldy than before.

She was panting when, at home, she sneaked a last anxious look at her canvas, which would take days to dry and become definitive, closed the shed door on it and resumed her second life as housemaid.

They breakfasted on porridge and tea. Clarice gave Father his tonic, and dusted till she had to sit on the stairs to stifle an impulse to weep. She felt dilapidated—could she too, like her father, be afflicted with unsteady nerves? Was she meant to inherit this, along with the weak heart? She laughed sorrowfully.

'Clarice?' Father called from the drawing room, where she had not yet collected his tray.

Who else?

'I'm dusting,' she replied, trying to sound as if she were a great distance away. She was never properly alone here.

In the kitchen, the stove soon made the dismal, cold air hot. The Beaumaris house had witnessed her graceless transformation into a poor and usually reluctant housekeeper. Before Father's retirement, they had enjoyed domestic help, or better, taken it for granted. Her parents were reserved when it came to talking about money, to talking about most things, really, but she gathered that their financial situation had been debilitated by copious medical expenses; they had both grown very reliant on doctors—Mum for her heart, Father for his nerves and arthritis. It was surely worse to have had and lost servants than never to have had the luxury. Growing up with it had ruined Clarice. She was a laughable cook, uninspired, incompetent, with no natural inclination. The vacancy of a kitchen.

She lost track while Father's beef tea custard was firming in its pan on the side of the stove—the brightening garden had held her eye at the window—and suddenly the water around the gelatinous yellowish stuff was boiling.

Her hands panicked, and she dipped one into the water. It was scalded. She felt a little sick but also vindicated by the knowledge that when the custard was turned out, there would be holes in it. Father would pout at them. She would have preferred the burning sensation on the back of her hand to be more violent; it helped to steady her mind. She prepared the pater a baked apple, as penance. He liked his sweets but could not stomach anything heavy.

Mum was reading in bed, avidly.

'Still having fun with your Somerset Maugham?'

She smiled a lovely, secretive smile. 'It's very entertaining. Did the painting go well?'

'Not too badly.' It was almost impossible to talk about her work, but she was rather touched Mum had asked. 'What do you fancy for pudding?'

Resting her book on her knee and lifting her eyes to the ceiling, Mum thought. She looked slightly anaemic. 'Maybe scones? The bran ones agreed with me last time.' Dr Broadbent had lately recommended Mum's conversion to wheatmeal and she was bravely embracing it. 'With jam? You don't want to sit here for a bit and chat?'

Clarice was restless; she did not think she would be able to abide sitting by her mother. Better misanthropy, solitude.

'I'll see about those scones.'

'Don't go to any bother, dear.'

This familiar phrase grated less than usual. She laid her hand briefly on the old head. 'I'll leave you be.'

She was stirring ginger cordial. Louise, swanning in on an impromptu visit, demanded a glass. Clarice realised she had been listening in a trance to the sound of the spoon against the jug, possibly for a while. She stopped stirring and surrendered the jug.

'Not enough sugar, Sis,' Louise concluded. 'You're lucky to be in here in the warm. The rest of the house is freezing!'

Louise disappeared and her barely audible chattering with their mother was pierced every so often by a shriek of laughter. Mum's cheeks would be pink after Louise went.

Drying her hands on her apron, Clarice went to put Chopin on the gramophone. She had purchased the record after hearing this music at Mrs Hamlin's party. Back in the kitchen, a fragment of music would suddenly present itself as a gift. Finished for better or worse with her chores, she would pass the time till the light started to fade, sewing old fur cuffs into the lining of Mum's slippers. She had read in a magazine that this gave a cosy effect. And then she would be away from here—painting.

Louise popped her head in again, saying she would give her kingdom for a hot cup. Clarice had no conversation in her; she only wanted to look at the garden and listen to her music, contemplating the gorgeous unease of last night.

Her sister was wearing some new provocative scent, animal-musky. Not even the second baby had taken away her style. She leaned coquettishly in the doorway, her life seeming a playful thing. The vermilion scarf slung over her shoulder threatened to fall. She was always preparing for a glamorous performance, her hips toying with the air they occupied.

'Gosh, I'd kill for a cup of tea.' Louise waited another minute before she reached for the kettle and filled it herself.

'Ouch!' She had plucked a hair off Clarice's head.

'Grey one. Well you *are* the older sister. Ha! Thirty-two. You should look after yourself a bit more. It starts to become important at our age.' Louise had been colouring her own hair for years. It was very dark, timeless. 'I could help you, if you want . . .' she trailed off meditatively.

'No, thank you.' The tiny prick of pain gave way to a discomforting raw feeling. 'Silver,' she said. 'Silver hair is dignified.'

'Yes, on a man.' Louise smiled. 'I agree. Quite seductive.'

'And on a woman, too, I find.'

Louise raised her eyebrows. 'That Carruthers from down the street—what do you think of him?' she asked brightly. 'He's pretty enough. One could do worse.'

Clarice hesitated. 'He's a boy.'

'A boy? *So?* That reminds me, Ron got bitten by a snake last night,' she tripped on, and Clarice felt herself melting into shadow behind the glare of her sister's talk, eclipsed. 'He came racing in from the yard on his toddler legs, crying, but Ted knew just what to do. He always knows. Somehow he calmed the little chap down and got him in the bathroom to wash the bite. He cut incisions through the puncture marks! Cut! Can you believe it? He only dared confess this later when the doctor had reassured me and I'd had a sherry.' She winked. 'I do like a drop. It relaxes me. I said, "You took a razor to the baby?" It was outrageously funny. We get on famously with the doc. After Ted did the cutting, he sucked out some of the blood and venom. The doc was so impressed. He said, "If everyone was like you, I'd be out of business." Ted really does have the coolest head I've ever seen.'

The tenacity with which Louise sang Ted's praises made Clarice think something was amiss, especially as the man hardly seemed to deserve it; he did not quite look at you when you were speaking, giving the unpleasant impression of being somehow underhanded or suspicious yet also fundamentally uninterested. Was Louise afraid her husband would leave her?

Steam was shooting up from the kettle. Louise did not notice—her demeanour was too regal. Clarice went through the motions, scalding the pot, spooning in plump spoonfuls of tea; she loved the earthy sweet fragrance.

'I didn't know what was going on. I was in our room. Ted had sent me off because I was wailing.' Louise had apparently doubled back on her story. 'I'm a protective mother to a fault, but I can't help it, can I? It's the instinct.' Clarice poured in the water and fitted the cosy. 'Ted took control of the whole situation. The little one was lying down getting tickled by the time the doc arrived. I was putting cold water on my face.'

Louise lifted a hand to her forehead, re-enacting. Clarice's own hands shook as she shaped the bran dough into circles; watching those fallible hands, she did not regret their actions in Arthur's van. What was he doing at this moment? She saw his lively, curious eyes—that open attention that separated him from the Teds of the world. She might tell her sister about him one day and give her a shock, but she did not feel like it now. The story of the snakebite, with its shifting chronology, was eternal.

'Ted went out and killed the snake to show the doc when he arrived. So they'd know which anti-venin. I haven't a clue how he found it—it was almost dark. Ron was tickled pink with his ligature.'

Clarice remembered, with exquisite clarity, an earlier moment from the night before: waiting for the first reel to start, her effervescent orange drink, a volcano-shaped mountain through a painted window, the organist arranging his coattails as the red velvet curtain was finally lifting; waiting.

15

She had been working at a view of the Yarra, and afterwards came by Meldrum's studio to get his opinion on it. She told herself that this was her intention in going there; however, she soon understood it had been different. These visits were always convivial, slightly formal, a way of showing him thanks and respect, and maybe also her maturity—the risks she was taking. Rather than a failure or a half-failure, she usually brought him a partial tentative success, something she was not quite sure of, in order to see it through his experienced, severe eyes. Perhaps now considering her an independent artist, he was more forthcoming with praise, though he was sometimes silenced too. Her style, it seemed to her, was every day more particular and more itself, unwilling to be tied to his or anyone else's method.

She wondered what he was painting. The last time she had seen any of his work was at the Group Exhibition. Some gum studies done at Eltham had fascinated her, aroused a kind of recognition. It did indeed appear that he was onto something new in those; he really was setting about remaking Australian landscape painting, making it, on its own terms, afresh. They were not grand, sweeping or studied but close, immediate, tight. One called *The three trees* had especially interested her. Hasty, even rough. Its insides almost showing. Like all Meldrum's work, it proclaimed: that is precisely what I saw, right there, then, without prejudice; *that and nothing else.* When your mind entered its skilful depth, you were in the pungent bush, fixing on it a vigilant, unwavering gaze. You smelled a little smoke from a camp, your own damp human heat and, engulfing it all, the absolute crispness of peppery, lemony, honeyed plant life; you bathed in bush light. The Eltham studies, of course, had been too analytical and naked for the critics.

His lesson had not yet finished—the class was busy with a still life of ginger jars. As ever, he had them fervent and only two, hearing the door, turned in her direction: a girl she did not recognise, and Arthur. Clarice and her lover had to be careful that no one notice any unusual familiarity between them. She generally avoided socialising with the group, yet here she was, arriving before the end of the lesson, for the ephemeral, distressing pleasure of a look at him. This, she abruptly realised, was the true reason for her visit. He stared at her for a matter of seconds and his eyes were back on his canvas; she preferred not to study it.

She stood silently at the back of the room. There were fifteen or so of them there, earnestly infantile or housewifely in their smocks.

'The optimal viewing distance for a finished painting will

usually be approximately twenty feet back, the same distance that separated the painter from his subject as he painted,' Meldrum was saying intensely. 'Otherwise it will not transmit the precise illusion of reality.' No one else could put *precise* and *reality* next to *illusion* with such unblinking confidence.

Yes, she thought, but you were not always after accuracy, exactly. Coming close to the painted surface—though it seemed incomprehensible, abstract—revealed the magic, the artifice, the art: the application of paint upon a flat plane capable of bewitching a viewer. She herself was bewitched, right then, by Arthur's statuesque form and the idea of his hands. To distract herself, she paid attention to the new girl.

Young, perhaps twenty. Later, Clarice would hear someone call her Jean; she would never know her. Jean did not distract her from Arthur. In fact, the girl somehow reflected Clarice's awareness of him. In a snug red jumper, Jean had an extreme prettiness, a childish yet flowered femininity. Her eyes were amused, opulent. She was delighted to be there, relieved to have turned at last into a bohemian. She kept turning to smile at Clarice, an irrepressible smile that seemed exaggerated and charming to Clarice, who was so practised at dissembling her own higher-pitched feelings. Jean's excited, joyously free rendering of the ginger jars showed she was famished for art. She would develop quickly as a painter.

A month or so after smiling back at Jean, Clarice read in *The Age* that the girl had been discovered dead. She would not develop as a painter. Jean had gone to the theatre with 'artist friends' (was the journalist implying that frequenting artists was itself a dangerous activity?), to see Bernard Shaw's *Pygmalion*. She went missing that night. After the play, someone saw her running for the train, giggling, and that was her friends' final view of her. She had been killed—a random, inexplicable attack, apparently, no meaning to hang from her death. Her spark extinguished like that. And one burgeoning artist, one bright-eyed young woman less to walk among them.

Clarice spent the best part of two days brooding over this passing of a girl she never knew; even when she was not thinking about it, she was thinking about it. It was odd. Was it just the surprise of the news? The incongruity? Jean and her ginger jars had been so promisingly vital. It was wrong that such a life force, such momentum should have been directed at death. This has to be Arthur's doing, Clarice thought; he leaves me too open. She wondered if to be open to love meant being open to death. And at that moment it dawned on her that all the thinking about Jean was also a way to think, finally, about Paul, her little brother, who had ended his own life in the asylum. She saw that Jean's death and Paul's were connected. They were the same, because one death is really all deaths—*is* Death.

She would never forget Mum coming in, still-faced, to announce it. At home in Casterton. Clarice was twenty.

'What is it?'

'I've had a telegraph. Your brother's died.'

She remained in her usual armchair for some unusual twisted moments, then floated to her feet. 'What?'

'Yes. Died.' Mum's voice was too full and awfully flat. She appeared to be postponing her reaction.

Clarice moved towards her. 'How?'

When she learned some years later of soldiers under the influence of shell shock, she recalled the silent frozen quality in Mum's face as she gave her the news.

So, he had done it himself. In her head, she kept repeating, as if it were a riddle: *by his own hand*. She was stupefied, but perhaps not wholly surprised. Before she felt sad for little Paul or for herself, she felt sad for Mum, because once she had let herself grasp this, it was unlikely she would be the same again.

Clarice had never pictured him doing it. That is, she had thought of a torn sheet and his white neck—so thin. But she had not allowed herself to come too close to the practicalities. After learning about Jean, her body face down, one leg in the gutter, her handbag missing and red jumper askew—no doubt the same jaunty red jumper she had worn that day under her painting smock—Clarice wanted the details of Paul's death. She required them. The facts of horror can be moreish: once you have started nibbling, though you may begin to feel sick, you discover in yourself a ghoulish appetite.

Now she re-created it mercilessly. Paul in pyjamas, pacing the room. His expression unemotional, quite impassive and adult in its resignation; precocious. Violet pools of fatigue under his eyes. An air of something—hard to define—gone irreparably wrong with him. Next the sheet. The sheet parting company from the narrow, ungiving bed. The tearing of the sheet, difficult at first, becoming easier, easy. The sound of tearing fabric, strangely penetrating and loud, as if it were more than just textile in nature, what was being rent.

The noose, his hands knowing what to do, demonstrating how it is done. See? Like this. It's not complicated. Such a bright boy. His hands beginning to shake, a kind of reflex. Then the cloth being tied to the upper bunk, the secure, simple knot, and the loop going over his head, over the perfect beautiful line of that incredibly soft-skinned neck. His fifteen-year-old, terribly soft neck, never kissed by anyone but their mother.

The moment before it was too late, time thundering in his ears; a furious sea in a shell. And the spasmodic moment after.

She did not imagine he thought of them much, at the end; he was always independent, his thoughts his own.

After having at last watched his death unfurl in pictures, known it, she went to Half Moon Bay to paint, hurrying to get there before the light changed. The work gave her some rest. When she had finished, she identified in her landscape something of the passing of time. Time, passing—a slow, viscous flow. A painting was a dream not of immortality but of mortality.

At home that night, she told Mum she meant to go to the art colony Meldrum was organising at Anglesea. A fortnight of camping; it would not be expensive. They would drive down in a convoy. She had had the offer of a place in Henry's car. Ada too.

'You'll have to ask your father,' she said.

'I'm going.'

'An art camp?' Was she put out?

'Yes. I must go.'

She studied Clarice and then, her tone shifting, coura-geous, said, 'I'll see what I can do.'

16

She approached the beach through a blackening mass of dense, stunted trees. It was nearly sundown. Oriented by the roiling noise of the waves and the old smell of salt, she followed a sandy path between trunks moulded into curves by the wind.

The beach. A long stretch of wet sand glowing silver, dark clumps of seaweed thrown by the water. Without being hard, the light was rather metallic, a slightly purple blue-grey that lent the cliff wall across the way a deep warmth, between red wood and caramel. The incoming waves were shockingly white, extravagant with the finest foam.

There was room here and her spirit expanded into it. She subsided onto the slope leading down to the beach, her fingers convulsively grasping a tuft of sharp spinifex. She was not thinking of Arthur, but her urge to paint resembled the tremulous restlessness of other sensual cravings. The light diminishing quickly, she unlaced her shoes, pulled them off and sat breathing hungrily, as hungry as a drunk guzzling liquor. Clarice would not paint that first night. She had to clear herself of home, let in the new air, freshen herself—she had to go vacant. After a while, she began to laugh, laughing till a ticklish pressure built in her skull and her own internal sea erupted, salt water running down her face.

She stood and wandered, giddy, barefoot, through the near dark, towards the rising tide.

17

Arthur was grateful but also unhappy she had come. His words and gestures were as smooth as ever. His stable exterior was undisturbed and this was probably all other people saw: the still lake of him by which you wanted to linger, reflected in that proud surface to advantage. But his turmoil was loud to Clarice; there was trouble in him. He had become a divided man, suspended between a lawful wife, the mother of his child, and a secret consort who mothered only painted landscapes.

They had found the odd hour together at Anglesea, but never a whole afternoon until the day Bella came down with a nasty cold that made her morose and unwilling to leave their tent. And he was liberated.

Out, as usual, since before sunrise, Clarice was returning to camp and human society, swollen with her art, vigorous and boyishly blithe. Not far from her tent, she caught sight of him.

'Hello,' he said warily, though he had been lying in wait. 'How are you?'

'Hello. I'm very well,' she replied, with similar delicacy. 'You?'

'Fine, fine.'

They could be adept at handling the uneasiness, like practised jugglers of asymmetrical objects, but later they would be clumsy and this was the nature of it: there was no clear progression, no security. It was after twelve by her wristwatch. Ada, who was only a short distance off, sketching a gum, had noticed their exchange; from her observant posture, her body even quieter than usual, Clarice thought she had deduced its meaning.

Did everyone at camp know? She tried to make her face superficial, but it was impossible to talk to a lover without displaying intimacy. Her face betrayed them by striving not to. During the years when she had waited for this intensity of feeling with a man, she had not foreseen how guilt could muddy it. She lifted her watch again, as if measured time might absolve them.

'Can I look?' he asked.

She was rather embarrassed by the morning's painting, not used to producing scenes so resplendent, so very unambivalent.

The light already hot, the sun was lifting over a beach. There was a touch of green, but you were mainly aware of a bright flood of oranges, reds, yellows—sumptuous colour soaking sky and sand, everything liquefied, no terra firma and the horizon irrelevant, arbitrary. A figure in a bathing suit stood to one side, long, thin, featureless, neither quite man nor woman, overwhelmed by radiance.

He would think it showed their coming together. It did, of course, and more particularly, her physical ripeness; it was all sensation, a sort of wholeness, a victorious flush. She had omitted guilt or ignored it and this made her blush, now, echoing the painting, but also making it sordid. There was no denying the thing had come from her. Arthur did not comment. After a moment, looking down at the hot canvas, he briefly described his idea. She consented immediately, avoiding thought, her head turned so that she could not see Ada. They would no doubt be missed. That was the price.

He waited a way off with folded arms and a vaguely studious attitude, while she went into her tent, supposedly for a cardigan in case it turned blowy but really to gather herself; crawling on all fours, she had a sense of alarm at not being able to predict the weather.

When she re-emerged, Ada was gone, having removed herself as unobtrusively as she had earlier filled the space. They saw no one else as they walked briskly along the clifftop path, away from camp and the beaches where most of the painters worked. It was important not to run into anyone. To someone watching from the beach below—seeing two silhouettes suddenly invading the frame of a landscape, hastening across it—if not recognisable, they would certainly appear furtive.

They kept up a strong pace for a time, marching dumbly along in an almost military fashion. Her shoes were covered in sandy soil, as if they had become extraordinarily old, relics. The sun burned her hands; the cardigan would be useless or she could put it under her head. Beyond the circle of her hat's brim was a great incandescence that was most intense over the ocean, which could not be stared into.

When they were distant enough from the campsite, they slowed. Their silence grew more comfortable but then somehow argumentative. Flirtatious.

She was dazed by the sun and had no idea where they would find shelter. The only vegetation was a low, thick marine heath unbroken but for the path. How long had the path existed? As far as she could see ahead, there was no change; nothing would offer concealment. On what was probably a fool's errand, they continued doggedly.

'I have to see you more,' he said at last, offering this impossibility with an irritable tone. 'I think of you constantly.'

'Did you expect you would stop thinking of me, after a while?'

'No. I didn't mean that.' He turned away and when he looked back at her his face was pink. They were both perspiring heavily. 'I never let myself expect anything.' He did not ask what she had expected or expected now. Perhaps he did not dare.

'You expected . . . nothing?'

'Oh, I don't know. But I'd do anything to be with you all the time.'

'Anything but.'

He grunted, but she was only stating, not reproaching him. She had never demanded anything, never been tempted to. There was no shared life to envisage. What they might have been together, out in the open, was hollow potential, a half-formulated question. Arthur had changed towards her: his opinion of himself was sullied; he had grown cynical.

'When I look down there at the water, I get a bit of vertigo,' he said angrily. 'I was afraid of heights as a kid. Less so as an adult, but it stays with you. I get it from my old mum, who had a pathological fear of them. She wouldn't even get up on a stool.' Reluctantly, he added: 'I'm nervous up here. Nauseous—I feel dwarfed.'

Clarice was interested. 'Dwarfed?'

'It's a sensation like being about to die.' He was quiet for a moment. 'How I imagine it, anyhow. Like thinking you're about to die.' He paused again. 'I've been coming here at night.'

'Why? Why did you want to come here today, then?'

'In the dark, it terrifies me. Even if I stay on the path, well back from the edge.'

Seeming a veiled message, this annoyed her. She could not stop herself. 'Martyrdom?'

'You must hate me and sometimes I hate you.' She thought he was both relieved and appalled to have blurted this. He waited a little too long before clarifying: 'I love you so much I hate you.'

She stopped walking. It was the first mention of love. 'We have a lot going against us, but we have an advantage. We have honesty. I prefer you to be horribly honest. You seemed so lucid to me, when I first met you.' It was hard for him, she knew. He was not a hypocrite: he was a free being restricted by a fully shaped life. He had a flair for improvisation which he was not at liberty to exercise.

He tried to draw her to him. She did not open her arms; she was not ready.

His hands fell to his sides. He said, 'You keep yourself apart.'

'Physically?'

'No—in all ways.'

But if she was aloof, it was not just because she was jealous of her privacy. It was also on account of Bella's face, which could appear in her mind, smiling a gentle elastic smile. A confusing vision that turned her cold; their physical bond should not have admitted this interference.

'Let's stay here,' she suggested, wanting to prove him wrong.

He was taken aback.

No one in view in any direction. It was not out of the question that someone might come along, but they were going to risk it. The alternative to taking risks was paralysis. She began to undress right there, fast, before she could think better of it. She stepped out of her skirt and laid it out on the path, ludicrously crouching to smooth it, as though it were a cloth on a table she was setting for a special occasion.

Arthur waited, but then he untucked his shirt. Clarice continued undressing under the harsh sun. She had not showed him her body completely before and never like this, in daylight. He watched her remove her underwear, exposing herself. She was curious about her own pale forms, the pinkish areas and the patch of dark hair. Her comically gangly knees. Her head cast a shadow when she looked down that gave her the feeling of being two people, one taller and foreboding. The hours of work had left her neck wooden. She loosened her hair. The air and sun on her nudity were dreamlike or potently real.

His face alert, he moved towards her, but she gestured for him to finish undressing. She sat down on her skirt, listening to the waves and half closing her eyes against the light's assault. There was titanium white on the fingernails of her left hand, cadmium yellow on a few matted strands of hair falling into her eyes. She felt strangely sure of herself, insightful.

Their accumulated time alone together over the past months did not add up to much. The handful of times they had been intimate, it had tended to begin beautifully, but her pleasure was painfully short-lived, anticlimactic. After, she retracted into herself.

Arthur's clothes were scattered haphazardly around him. Even naked, he held himself confidently. His body was compact. She looked at it, at his silky shoulders and muscular, imposing hands, solid legs and slender buttocks, brown neck and face, long, unexpectedly delicate feet and queer, soft masculinity. He remained unknown. A pattern to be puzzled over.

He sat opposite her cross-legged, with a pleasant sort of pride, but needing her approval. They were both rather stunned and incredulous to find themselves in this situation. She chuckled. His discontent had receded to somewhere remote, letting him be childlike.

He grinned hesitantly and lowered himself with clownish gravitas so that he lay on the earth, drawing her down with him. She acquiesced, finally, and stretched out, though when he brought his body over hers, she shifted away. She wanted them to lie side by side. This disoriented him. She cupped her hand against the side of his face to shade his eyes; they were both half blinded by sun. Squinting hard, she found a trace of his work—burnt umber on his cheekbone. Her artist. She kissed his temple fondly as if they were old lovers, their bodies entirely accustomed to mutual adoration and coupling.

'What did *you* paint today?'

'Hm? Oh, those rock formations at the end of the beach.'

'And?' He was hard on his own efforts; she had to inquire about them discreetly.

'I was floundering around. Thinking about you. I'm always scared you won't like what I do.'

As she had done with Herb, she tried to avoid commenting on his art. 'I do like what you do. Your landscapes have weight to them.' He was a new painter, but some of the authority that surrounded him in his public life, that lawyerly clout, maybe, was finding its way onto his boards. He too had not been able to resist starting early on landscapes. His scenes were straightforward, grounded. You felt their materiality. Or she felt it because she was his lover, her body knowing the hands that had made them. His skies, though, were not convincing—he never really took grey on and his clouds were small and well behaved. So your eyes stayed low in those earthly landscapes.

'I'd love to make you happy,' he said.

'You can't paint to make people happy.'

'Can you make people happy with love?'

'You'd like to think so. I don't know.'

Their skin was roasting and this might have been true freedom, nakedness against a backdrop of breaking waves. Modern life appeared to have been obliterated and they were reduced—or was it enlarged?—to simple inhabitants of nature. She would have liked all her skin to peel right off, to be a blinking newborn animal. This, she thought, could have been what attracted her to him: he tugged her down, as his paintings did the eye, into her body, her animal self.

Though he had not hurt her, there had been moments in their lovemaking at Anglesea when she had sensed Arthur barely holding himself back from brutality; rage simmered in him and her sensibility was repelled, could not link with his. She was stranded in the wasteland between her fantasies and the world they moved in. Reality became thin, full of holes.

But that afternoon in the sun, perhaps because they understood that this could not last much longer, their minds were soft and able to lean in the same direction. Pressing her thumbs to his hipbones, she kissed him again, on the mouth, and desire twitched awake in her.

Her eyes were open, which was new. She had never looked into the face of sexual pleasure for more than a moment or two, unsettled by how it undid the countenance. Watching Arthur now, she saw him unstitched. Still thinking coherently, though not for long, she marvelled at this liberation, the discarding of the pretence of integrity. It seemed that in love, if you were fearless enough, you could admit you were coming apart—you could come quite apart.

He was beaded with sweat, bright and astounding. Ambitious, afraid, mortal. And she saw it all split wider open, her own consciousness narrowing to a taut tunnel; the jolt of the end ended nothing and everything. The sun was soporific and hot, as hot as the colours in the painting that had foretold or conjured this.

Darkness. Darkness perfumed with salt and some unidentifiable green growth. Heat, all through her skin.

The sun had set; Clarice panicked. 'Arthur!' She shook him. 'Arthur, we fell asleep!'

He clutched at her with a truncated groan, then shrank away and was on his feet. His body in the dark, driven by fear, was still graceful.

Her heart had accelerated uncomfortably and she clambered onto her knees. There seemed to be live flames running beneath her skin; it was sore to touch—she realised that their tanned hides would be a kind of scarlet letter. He was dressing chaotically, half asleep. The quiet wellbeing was fractured.

'How long do you think we slept?'

She tried to make sense of the garment she was holding. 'A long time, by the look of it. I don't know how we could have.'

Once dressed, they straightened each other up as best they could, brushing off invisible sand. Then they were almost running, retracing their steps. It was a long and unfamiliar journey back. They stumbled here and there, breathless, mortified. At last, the camp was close.

Stopping, they listened. From the rumble of voices and tinny clatter of pots and pans, dinner was being prepared.

He hissed, 'We can't go straight back. I left the car down at the beach. I'll have to go for it. I'll say . . .' He exhaled heavily. 'I'll say I took a siesta and just woke up.'

'Well, that would be true,' she said, befuddled, unable to decide if this was an adequate excuse. 'What will *I* say if someone sees me?'

'Lord.' He was flailing. 'I don't know. I don't know if we should split up here.' She did not want to. They were fully awake and entirely concentrated now, yet their mental faculties remained groggy, uncooperative. 'Why don't you come down to the beach with me? I'll drive you back, drop you off at the road near camp. If anyone sees you getting out, we'll say I passed you on the road. You wandered off sketching and lost track of time. That's believable. Maybe better than being seen coming back from this direction. In the dark.'

'Is it believable?' The plan seemed illogical, though she could not put her finger on why. She was silent for a moment. 'I don't have my sketchbook.'

'It doesn't matter. Everyone'll be around the fire eating, anyhow. No one will notice us arrive. I'll go and see'—he sighed again—'how she is.'

'Bella.'

'Yes. And you'll go and join the others. Or wait for a bit in your tent first. Whatever you want.'

Whatever she wanted. They gave the camp area a wide berth, at one point suddenly glimpsing the vivid light of the fire from which they were exiled and distinguishing loud, jokey voices. The voices dropped as someone started singing a song in Spanish. An ardent, revolutionary song. Clarice and Arthur moved away from the music. For several awkward minutes, they were a little lost among unfathomably twisted trees. But they found their way down—miraculously, never once losing their footing—and came out not far from the river that led like an elegant arrow to the sea.

They strode by the estuary, eyes on the larger body of water they were approaching; it looked utterly black and enormous. The tide had come in, the waves arriving fast and furious. She had a flash of horror. The estuary by day did not quite reach the sea and it was easy to cross from the camp side to the long beach over a generous expanse of sand; she adored it there then, a boundless middle place between land and water, damply shining.

Now, sunset over and night begun, there was no dry route across. The rising tide had sought out the little river and claimed it.

'Oh,' Arthur muttered.

It would have taken too long to go back to the road and follow it around to the beach. Far too long. Staring into the obsidian ocean, she was dismayed; her imagination slid into a lightless region.

'Difficult to judge the water,' she said.

'It's very shallow, I think. We'll run?' He was begging, as if suspecting she would refuse.

'We'll run,' she agreed, but she would have to act immediately.

She took off, feeling fatalistic and bizarrely balletic.

They stayed close to each other, without holding hands. Arthur and Clarice were not united anymore and bore no resemblance to old lovers. They were separate entities on the run, fleeing back to civilisation, to the present. He was right: the water only came to their ankles, but the terror that followed her as she ran into the dark, cold water, into the unthinkable, imprinted itself on her soul. The euphoria, too.

18

Some questions were quelled, others left echoing. The brush jumped in her hand like it was of her own flesh. It was important to stop at this first, tenuous sign of calm, as the board was taking charge of itself, not the product of chance, but always meant to be this way. Her spine straight and exultant, she contemplated the results critically. She had returned to paint the sandy in-between place she and Arthur had seen reclaimed by water. Now it felt inviolate; the tide had barely begun to advance.

'You scared me.' He had come up on her from behind.

A child was sitting a way down the beach, but Arthur's arms came around her all the same. They had been heedless since they woke burnt-skinned under the night sky. He sought her out as often as he could and came to her tent each night. People knew, though no one was saying anything to Clarice's face; they were not unkind, but amused, perhaps, looking deep into her eyes, or disappointed, avoiding them. She had suddenly become very human to them and this was looked down on. There was much talk of a new, more open morality, new ways of living, but beneath this, they remained conservative, their Victorian values firmly entrenched. She did not enjoy being an object of attention. However, their disapproval did not sting as much as she would have expected. The attitudes of others seemed to be becoming less important. Bella was the exception, of course. Arthur maintained that she did not know. 'She would never believe it of me,' he said once, staring at his feet. His wife was keeping to her bed, sick with the cold that would not go away.

Clarice stretched her left arm that had endured a crooked position so long, holding palette and brushes. She was beginning to wilt.

He did not apologise for startling her, but said, 'You work so quickly.'

Still and reverential, he looked at her painting. There might have been a slight, competitive tension in him.

It was a sunset view of the place they stood in. This and her painting of the hot sunrise were companion pieces, she thought, holding possibilities and progressions between them; they formed a whole. They might be some culmination for her. She needed to believe it. Today's painting was less victorious. The pink cast onto clouds and sea by the lowering sun—out of the frame—was a final-hour warmth.

The prelude to night was breezy. She closed her eyes so she would not see that scene anymore and also to smell Arthur better; she wanted to commit his smell to memory. She recognised the odour of his van and perhaps a little of

Bella's lavender eau de cologne. His fingers were against her ribs and, just as strongly as this, she could feel the wet board to which she had been joined for hours, though she was no longer touching it either with brush or with gaze.

'Will you give it to me? Can I have it?'

'You always want them.' She opened her eyes. 'How would you explain it?' She stepped out of his arms. 'It's for my exhibition, anyway.'

She stared the painted scene into meaninglessness, a void. The sea darkened behind it. Arthur took out his tobacco and papers and began the slow rolling of a cigarette. A distance off, the child, until then seated, unfolded, elongated and became kinetic: a small figure running away from the beach. Clarice noticed in herself a growing interest in the human form; perhaps physical love did that to you.

'She helped me clean my brushes before,' she said. 'Her name is Sonia. She was watching the ocean all afternoon. She'd pick up things we don't—things we've forgotten to see.'

'Maybe. This is frighteningly close to utopia. Are you coming to dinner, then?'

'I'm starving.'

'You have to keep your strength up, with the way you work.' He liked to think of her eating.

'I'd stay out here forever.'

He touched her wrist and held it loosely. His grip softened and released. 'Can I help you clean up?' His eyes searching for a rag.

She was already opening her turpentine, its perfume like a scream. 'No. I'm fine.'

He turned away.

'Productive day?' she asked his back.

'I was just messing around.' He had withdrawn. 'I'll see you.'

She hesitated. 'I'll be along shortly. And I'll see you after.'

Nights in Clarice's tent, they tried to muffle their incoherent voices by stuffing balled clothing between their teeth; she felt like an animal, not wild and free anymore but tamed, a docile horse chomping on its bit, or like some prisoner, bound and gagged. Once she accidentally reached for her stockings—their tint was called *Rose Morn*—which tasted of the powder she had dusted on her legs and were oddly elusive in her mouth. Other times, they silenced themselves with their hands (whose hand over whose mouth?), as if this were not love but suffocation, a shared demise just averted. Even muted, the noise made the night crack down the centre. Tilting her head and lowering her lashes, she could almost see the shards of the broken night, the glittering of their slicing edges.

Once, Arthur jerked the fabric from her lips, determined to hear.

Her involuntary cry astounded her.

When she was breathing quietly again, she observed that the wind had lifted and rain pattered against the tent; there was going to be a downpour. She pulled a twig from under the sleeping bag where it had been worrying at her and, for comfort, stroked her own arm with it.

'You'll get rained on,' she told him. 'Stay a bit longer.'

'Right-o.'

Arthur wanted her to look at him. She would not. He had said that this place was almost utopia. Indeed it was. They had the holy trinity of art, nature, love. But their love had become a public spectacle, and now when Bella's face appeared in her mind, it was graver, a touch ashen. Surely she knew. Could she be oblivious, really? The camp was paradise, both before and after the shameful knowledge of nakedness. The very intensity of it made Clarice wonder if whatever they were to one another could last, if this were not a desperate holding on to something that could not be held.

19

Ada was painting very near the place where she had thought she would set up her own easel. Attempting a stealthy retreat, Clarice heard her name called out.

'Hello,' she said demurely.

'I'm not in your spot?'

'Not at all. I was just heading over there.'

'Would you like to see what I'm doing? I'd love to have your opinion.'

'Yes, of course.'

For the first time, with a strangely soft feeling, Clarice saw what the others meant when they said Ada copied her. The half-finished board, quite light, had an airiness she almost knew. The painted landscape did not show the real but gave a *sense* of it. The gentle pinks and oranges were familiar, as were the apparent looseness and the concealed restraint. It was evident, however, that a hand other than her own had done it. Perhaps Clarice could have, some years earlier, in another life. Noticing the board's potential, she felt a certain egotism.

'It's beautiful,' she said. 'I wouldn't do anything differently.'

'Really?' Ada turned, smilingly confused, gushing, 'I can't believe I showed you. I admire you so much.'

She was disturbed by the idea that Ada might not continue painting, might abandon it, as so many did, when it was such an aid for survival. And she could have talent—whatever that was. Suddenly stern, she said, 'You shouldn't be self-deprecating. You're committed to your art, aren't you? Willing to take it as far as you can?' The girl may have been of a kind whom doubt would limit rather than galvanise; worse, she was intelligent and would probably realise it. Clarice gazed at her a little furtively, as if staring at doubt.

Ada did not sidestep; her pleasure over Clarice's approval left her unguarded. 'I don't know,' she said. 'It's hard for me. You make it appear easy.'

Clarice snickered. 'I'm sorry if I gave you that impression. It can be torture, actually. Of course, I don't compare the suffering to . . . the real suffering of a soldier, say . . .' Though, sometimes, she did. 'It's a delicate kind of torture,' she said, wanting to send herself up. 'Tiring. Discouraging, often. You hate yourself and then you start again. You mustn't waste any time admiring me.' She looked at her hands, at her trolley that would soon reveal what it was hiding. 'The easy part is the way you go somewhere . . . *else*, where you can be,' she grappled, her eyes moving to the water, 'if not your true self—I think I said that once, I was clumsy—then merge with some sort of truth. *Merge*. *Truth*. How grand. Just in flashes. When I say easy, I mean a relief.'

Something happened with the light that distracted them, a darkish opal gleam as the sun made its withdrawal felt. When she looked into Ada's face again, it was fragile and thoughtful and Clarice regretted never having invited her to the house or sought her out; but she did not really do friendship, not like that. It had to be very spacious.

'I'd been hoping we'd get a chance to chat,' Ada said. 'We hardly ever see you. Except from a distance, when you're working.'

'At a distance, working.' She laughed. 'That's my natural state.' She had the distinct impression that Ada knew about Arthur and did not judge her.

'I'm still boiling about that blasted review.'

'Oh, yes. *The lady has no right* . . . It'd slipped my mind.'

They both laughed briefly, but somewhere the conversation had taken on a mournful atmosphere. There was a silence.

'Galleries should be buying your paintings, not just friends,' Ada complained.

Clarice imagined this happening, dreamed of it, though only at night, when her visions were more grandiose or desperate. Such ideas never occurred to her on a beach. But she realised now there must have been gossip about who was and was not buying her work.

Ada made as if to put her hands on her hips, then thought better of it. The paintbrush in her right hand had the cheeky elegance of a cigarette holder; slight and unassuming, she was elegant. 'You don't paint as a Lady Painter should.' She had said it before, on the phone.

Clarice glanced again at the board, which became more magnetic, the more you looked; it undeniably had something. 'Nor do you.'

After a moment, Ada said, 'You have to leave your mark.'

She did not understand: whose mark? How so? And then she grasped it. 'For posterity? In the annals of art history?' She was laughing and they laughed together again, better this time, though there was still that sombre edge; they met each other's eyes.

'When you stray from flowers,' Clarice told Ada, 'when you turn your back on decoration and try to find your own way out here, you're done for. As far as *They* are concerned.'

'But you keep on.'

'You keep on. Ada, you have to.'

20

On the second-last day of the camp, he wanted to take her on a bushwalk. She accepted. It was after lunch, in the space between her two painting sessions, a drowsy lull during which many of the others napped.

He knew the trail, having done the walk before, alone. Arthur could not get enough of nature; it never sated him— they had this in common. They set off by a farm, skirting the property, then crossing one of its fields before picking up a stream. It guided them into the bush. Three kangaroos were reclining by the stream, princely and unperturbed. She liked the leisurely shapes of them and their fuzzy, warm colour.

Quickly, as if she and Arthur had drifted to sleep and dis-covered themselves in a dream, they entered a rainforest's low, dappled light. And he began to tell the romantic story of a white man who had lived with native people around those parts. They were walking single file, Clarice behind, so she missed the odd detail. She was also distracted by the forest—it seemed to be some peculiar blend of outdoors and indoors. It was very moist, luxuriously green and dis-armingly close; secret. She was floating along a shaded yet luminous corridor between walls upholstered in bark, moss, leaf. This curiously internal nature amazed her; there was something to be learned from it. Arthur's story was another sort of corridor and she floated through it too.

Well over a hundred years before, William Buckley escaped from a convict settlement in Sorrento. He was found on the brink of starvation by the Wathaurong people, who accepted him into their tribe, thinking they recognised in him one of their own warriors come back from the dead. Buckley lived among the Wathaurong people for thirty-two years. It was powerfully attractive, this idea of an impris-oned man escaping captivity and flourishing in nature, amid native men. She was envious, and wondered about the influ-ence on the mind of never leaving a forest, of living enclosed in its myriad greens and wet arboreal air.

By the waterfall called Phantom Falls, she stood on a flat river boulder and stripped off her clothes. She was getting efficient at this, almost cocky. She crouched and lay back on the cool, eroded rock, staring at a patch of tree-hemmed sky. Everything leaned against the unbroken music of water thrown from a great height.

Arthur approached her. He was learning to wait, start-ing to understand the rhythms of her moods or at least to calmly accept them. Hands on his hips, he gazed down. The redness of his skin was sobering into a tan that gave him a dramatic air of wisdom, of life lived. She had to choose between watching him or the sky. She reached for his hand

and pulled him down, to have both. Their bodies, demanding, combative and slow to yield, fused on a black stone bed
in the middle of a river. Later, would her fingers find blood
along the ridge of her back?

They did not. And this was fitting and unsettling.
There had been a feeling of fantasy to the urgent, ungentle
coupling. She and Arthur might have been primordial beings
or gods, essences rather than people, distillations of spirit. If
she was right to suspect that he could not continue for long
to live so divided, that such strong sensation could not be
sustained, then soon, they would be making love only in the
back rooms of her imagination, where the cuts and haemor-
rhaging were intangible. This time seemed already to have
arrived. The moment was too exotic and sharply defined,
still, somehow, in its violence; it had to be an illusion, magic
of the mind. As they moved in the multicoloured light, her
eyes latched onto a green like the mossy green of Bella's soft
or soft-seeming dress. She shut them, after a while.

Rainforest. *Rain forest*. The paired words like the heart's
twin drum beats. Rain forest. Forest of rain, a sublime, completely unrelenting image.

After Anglesea, her rabidly nostalgic memory reached over
and over for their bushwalk. She preferred remembering
this to Flinders Street station. Their last conversation.

It was some weeks later. The platform was nearly empty
and the creamy sky was cryptic and cold. Her ears were
freezing. His hands turning nervous, Arthur was explaining

that his life with Bella was a good one. Even. Without certain highs and lows. Ever so good.

'Good?'

He did not speak of his daughter; he never did. He likened his married life then to a domestic garden. Tended, nurtured over the years. A symbiosis. A contract. She had not asked that he choose between his family and her, had not demanded justifications. She understood but detested this talk of the garden, its civilised tepidness. The choice it implied—of comfort over passion. The correct choice, for him, no doubt; she did not dispute it. He was trying to be open, talking this way—though, suddenly, she was tired, wearied by justifications and the apologetic, hangdog shifting of his hands. Her ears, her body was growing colder and colder in the unreadable light; it was that cold that alarms the blood into a retreat, resembling burning. He wanted their 'friendship' to continue. When he said *friendship*, she found that she could not remain near him. She could no longer stand to provoke in him such guilt. At times, the guilt had seemed to spread by contagion, from him to her; at others, to originate in herself. She saw that only in ending it would they have peace, be done with this turbid compromise.

'We mustn't see each other again,' she told him, smoothly, carefully, gauging his shock.

For a moment, he appeared to hold his breath. She felt a blockage in her own chest and the old pull towards him— fainter now. He knew she was right. She would have said something more had she been sure it would not have come out surly or stricken. Why should it be such a treacherous thing, the showing of emotion? And when and how to show it a matter of such complexity that it froze you? She might have given him more. She offered a face as impenetrable as the sky.

At Anglesea, the end had been approaching. But their love had always contained a fatal flaw, the suspicion of immorality. Perhaps passion always did.

Someone had insisted Bella stand with them for the photograph Arthur took on the day of Mrs Hamlin's party. Probably she would have preferred not to, because she came out looking distracted. Clarice never did discover just how much his wife knew, though she had believed Bella *knew*. Clarice kept the photograph in the drawer of her bedside table. They stood together, a motley crew joined by their commitment to tone, the conviction that this was the key to sight: the life of a subject was in the mingling of light and shade. In her own face, joy. She could not have hidden it from Arthur, who was watching from under the camera's dark skirt. She would not pretend to be depleted when she was full, her ecstasy having no tolerance for the usual duplicities.

She had used to picture a moment between Arthur and Bella, when the penny had dropped for her.

Oh. Our love is beyond resuscitation.

And another moment when, looking at Arthur, Bella saw that someone else had filled him up right to the brim with new life.

This is what Clarice had imagined. It had made her unhappy and also gleeful. But it was not wise to make assumptions about what people saw or understood, suffered or were indifferent to; it was surprising what could be missed. And most likely, it had not gone the way she had thought between Bella and Arthur at all.

She cherished the photograph, thinking of the French term *chéri* that began the word cherish, with its hint of bed-warmth and sweet red fruit. Or she resented its thinness, its cool surface and hard edges for being the only niggardly embodiment of him—on so many nights—to fill her hands.

He did not, of course, appear in the photograph. He merely haunted it in the haunting way of absence, as intimately and invisibly as a maker haunts his creation. He was its gaps and hollows, its longing and its emptiness.

THREE
Seascape

21

Years, looked back on, could concertina flat, as if there had not been any space or breath in them, no fluctuating light, no atmosphere. No jubilation, desperation or shifting chameleon states of mind. No contemplation of the moment.

It was the case too that, from outside, a woman's life not furnished with a husband and child rearing would appear bleak, brittle, to most. In a magazine that Louise had left at the house, Clarice read an article by a famous author on how the fight for women's freedom had gone too far. Men, he believed, had been left emasculated, without faith in themselves, because women had no faith in them, fought them, would not give up fighting for freedom. She had not really been able to make sense of the anxious argument. It was logical to her that if freedom was fought for, then this was the result of it not as yet having been won—not being secure and able to be counted on. She did not recognise herself here. When she thought of freedom, she thought first of the freedom to paint. If she had turned her eyes away from the common shape of a woman's life, it was in order to fight her true opponent: her art. The author found the Woman of today an unhappily severe creature, with her brief attire, short hair and aggression, a kind of soldier, and hers an unfulfilled, impoverished femininity. He clearly did not believe that a fighter, a soldier, could be enriched by her own cause.

She was continually surprised by the confidence with which many were ready to determine the self-fulfilment of others. With bemusement or exasperation, she realised that in the dozen or so years after it ended with Arthur, little happened to her that most would have considered eventful. But those were fertile, full years, with a fullness eluding words, as fullness does. Years dense with work for which her paintings would have to speak, if they could; if someone would listen.

A person she had not seen in a long while would ask, with a little tragic frisson, 'Clarice, my dear? How have *you* been?' Telling her she was indeed judged a sorry, reclusive figure, an object worthy of compassion. If you dedicated yourself to observation, you were viewed as isolated and sorrowfully inert. An outrageous misconception. Seeing what there was to be seen was far from passive; having your eyes and self open was surely the opposite of isolation—how could you be more connected to life? She and Herb had discussed this once, many years ago, before he left for the Continent.

'Active contemplation!' he exclaimed, triumphantly.

'Precisely,' she said, feeling they had a lot in common.

*

She completed hundreds, thousands of canvases and boards; a good deal more boards, which were cheaper. She got them, along with all her materials, from W & G Dean, in the city; they gave her a special price, understanding that those were hard times for artists, for almost everyone, of course, and sometimes even threw some in for free, bless them. The walking—journeying through landscapes on foot—was inseparable from the art. She was so much on the move, there being so much ground to cover. At night, she went home to cook, eat and sleep in her parents' house, but that was only her official residence, her domicile fixe, because in reality, she inhabited the outdoors. She was a wanderer. A nomad.

Returned from her travels, her shoes would be thick with dust; upturned, sand rained from them. In bare feet, she winced to take a step. Blood pounded in her feet and the bones of them felt tender; she examined with pride the sturdy calluses that clung to her big toes as barnacles cling to a pier. In bed, her left hip or right knee turned fretful. Asleep, she dreamed of walking. She drifted along Flinders Street, or made her way languidly over sand, as if walking through water. Her trolley sometimes figured in her dreams, but instead of being drawn along behind her, it usually hovered in the air above, like an overgrown balloon on a string or an odd cloud she was suspended from. She was so grateful for walking she almost felt guilty, as though the men on crutches or in wheelchairs, their mobility incomprehensibly disrupted by war, were reproaching her for glutting herself on smooth movement. On rare occasions, however, feeling a kind of kinship with the disrupted men, she thought of her trolley as a prosthetic limb.

She was promiscuous in her looking, wanting to see everything. Every caress light bestowed on the city and the people it sheltered and exposed. Many of these were exposed, destitute. Disenchanted. Passing silently among them, she sometimes felt like a shade, only she was very much alive, with her robust body and toughened feet, and obscenely fortunate. Perhaps, on occasion, when she painted a landscape bare of people, it was in fact a sidelong portrait of a person she had spied on the street.

She venerated streets and roads, however modest. They refused inertia, being an opening, a kind of door, always saying, 'You see, things could go this way. Or that.' And the motorcars that circulated in them, with their lovely silhouettes, boxy or aerodynamic. A certain Mr Fitzhugh, a critic who wrote for *The Argus* and seemed not to disapprove of her, conceded that no other artist had portrayed the motorcar as she had, with a sort of harmonious beauty. She took this as a terrific compliment. Motors were a blessing. Even the dangerous smell of their petrol exhaust was magnificent, as it mixed with the other loud ingredients in the scent of the city's life, the potent heat of carthorses, or men in the dole queue who were sleeping rough, the coal smoke lifting from factory boilers against the slow falling of birds.

The buildings, to her mind, were close, inscrutable friends, who turned splendid or a little sinister at nightfall, when they tossed light across the sleek Yarra. Those dribbles of light were a coded message that would always be beyond her grasp. Studying it, she was content—in her deep ignorance, in the long reverie before a revelation—and could have remained by the river indefinitely, herself a night reflection trembling towards dissolution. She could not stay out after dark as often as she would have liked, Father insisting she be back by a Reasonable Hour, but at calculated intervals she transgressed. She followed the electric lights along the night's confidential passageways, into its velvet volumes. Sometimes, she passed a place like the Latin Café, where there might have been people she knew or had known, a cluster of Meldrum's former students hotly debating art and philosophy. An odour of beer leaked out. Some jazz, perhaps. If a bearded, shaggy type whom she recognised emerged into the street, she looked quickly away. She only wanted to watch and, in this way, to take the city's pulse.

By squinting at the circle of light in a street lamp, you transformed it into a many-pointed star. Under the headlamps of passing motors, telegraph wires were revealed, briefly, as the silver threads of a great spider web. And there was the clean, fresh privilege of mist. Melbourne in the mist. Tucked between substance and mirage, her city of shifting presences. There was surely nowhere else more alluringly ghostly. She seldom felt alone. Clarice and Melbourne were joined; the paintings of her city were love poems, a consummation.

22

Maybe her friendship with Herb remained where others did not because it was easeful, each of them on a different side of the world, years elapsing without any word, and then a letter arriving and never any resentment for the silence. The understanding that you were living as you had to live and would be in touch when it was appropriate. She had had two letters from him during the war, not long after he left. The first announcing his decision to enlist. This was his latest adventure, the most recent chapter in his quest for experience; it would give him material for his art. She had recognised the tone, as light and carefree as his mood on those fresh mornings at Half Moon Bay. The second had arrived from his life as a soldier, though it did not evoke this. Chipper but tense, accelerated, it described a visit to Paris during a break from service; she had not found Herb there as she had known him. Long passages elaborated on the enchantments of Paris, but one section complained of the bathroom in the small hotel where he had lodged.

He had written:

What was sold as a bathroom is the dirtiest, most squalid and suffocating place you could imagine. And you know I have lived in a caravan and don't have fancy tastes. The strangest thing is the tub. If you can call it that. I've never seen such a tiny bath in my life, by a long shot. More of a sink. You wouldn't have believed it. I got in, but as I should have known from the unpromising appearance, it wasn't made to fit a human. I don't know what it was made for, really. Once I was wedged in, with my legs jammed against the sides, I thought I'd never get out again. I thought I'd have to call for help. You didn't know whether to laugh or cry. I'm not even long-legged.

It seemed to her that there was something poignant and unspeakable in this. And she would have liked to comfort Herb. She felt a little ashamed for being remote from her friend, from world events, from the war. She pictured the war so inadequately. Not able to bring the pictures to life, she could not keep her attention on them long. She waited some time and then replied with a short, insufficient note that finished with the postscript:

Your depiction of the bathtub horrified me. How atrocious. Charging good money for a room like that should be illegal. I hope you are putting it behind you.

He might have found her flippant.

Another letter, fourteen years later. This time, amid the

strangeness of letters, she recognised something of Herb. She penned a reply quickly, the words storming out.

Dalgety Road
Beaumaris

Dear Herb,

I'm glad to hear you've been prolific. Me too. There's no better feeling—or, at least, few forms of happiness to rival that one. The art you saw on your last trip to Paris sounded marvellously peculiar and heady and foreign and I love the idea of your gentle golden light there in the south. I can feel it from your description—so warming. Have you really laid down roots in Provence? Don't you ever miss The Bay? I must say I'm not much inclined to budge from Melbourne, though I will seem the yokel to you, alongside your European dalliances.

She wondered if this odd chatty woman in the letter could be the result of being too much in her own company. Most of her daily talk being of the functional, domestic kind, she had lost the habit of real conversation—and were letters not supposed to create the illusion of a conversation? There was no Clarice to offer but a distortion; she could not bring herself far into the wavering, deceptive light of language. She continued:

But I think of Corot, who found he had to return endlessly to the same subjects. I too have a notion that I must master what I have in front of me before I can go elsewhere. Master?

Ha! One tries, manages, within one's limited capacities. Any-
way, I suspect a landscape can never truly be mastered, never
domesticated nor wholly known, no matter how many times
you paint it. I've become philosophical.

I also have been busy, wearing out my shoe leather fast
and getting around in quite a scraggly state. Lately, we've been
buffeted by wild, breathtaking storms. At Half Moon Bay last
night—our old haunt—a violent wind had the clouds speed-
ing and the waves so ferocious that the spray was lashing me
as I stood sketching. A few hours later, back at home, I sensed
stillness and went out into the yard. The sky had cleared—com-
pletely—and the moon, high and almost full, was amazingly
salient. It seemed to have been drawn on, with great precision,
with some celestial, impossibly luminous ink. As the household
was asleep, I couldn't resist. I threw on coat and hat and ran
down to the Beach Road. It was cold, that Melbourne cold that
comes as a solid shock, then tingles, then aches, and makes
your exhaled breath seem a spirit friend—you've probably for-
gotten it, you traitor. The ocean was brooding but becoming
pacified moment by moment. It grew misty. I realised there was
no sensation left in my extremities. I'd been there some time. I
was so happy.

You ask after my parents.

She hesitated.

The week before, she had come back from town one day
to the smell of smoke. Following a faint milky streamer of
it around the side of the house, she found, at its origin, her
father, standing over a small fire. His face, tilted down into

the flames, absorbed some of their yellow. Somehow, she knew what was happening.

A painting was burning. He was doing it.

She asked what was going on.

'I'm clearing out the shed. There's no room left in it.' He insisted: 'It's overflowing.'

She hurried to the shed. Its door was open but had not been tampered with. She always kept it locked; it was her corner of private territory. It appeared that, by some bizarre accident, that day she had not locked it. It was true there was no room left in there. It had become a great struggle to close the door: she had to lean all her weight against it. And she was forced to store new paintings in her room, under the bed, on top of the closet and in every available spot. Mum had said, shaking her head, 'One day, you'll wake up floating on a sea of landscapes.'

Clarice had returned to the fire. She was a little peaky from the smoke or the unexpected emotion, but when she saw what it was he was burning, she collected herself; she became almost casual. Fortunately, he had initiated the proceedings with that old portrait of Louise. Louise's nearly black eyes gazed placidly from the flames. Clarice had never been fond of that painting. She had made Louise too sweet and sisterly. Those eyes not properly irresistible, too staid.

'I think that's enough arson for today,' she told Father, with a steely smile. Curiously, she had the upper hand. 'I see your point about the shed. It does need clearing out, but it's no concern of yours.'

He blinked, off-guard. Now that she was getting used to

the situation, it was not so much rage in her, not exactly, but more a tension released. As if she had always known he had this destruction in him, this denial, and he had simply made explicit something that had long gone unspoken between them.

She went for a bucket of water and doused the little holocaust. When she turned, he had gone.

They had exchanged no further words on the subject. She did not tell her mother about it, not wanting to worry her. She had been sleeping at the time. Perhaps Mum's poor health affected Father more than he let on. It seemed to Clarice, too, that his own ageing was a surprise to him. He walked stiffly, as though on new legs he had not yet got the hang of; it was no doubt in part the arthritis.

After this, she had entrusted the bulk of her paintings to Mrs Hamlin, who was delighted to take them into her care, clearly considering this a Task of Great Importance. Her son came to collect them in a van on three consecutive days and each time Clarice saw him off depleted, as if sending beloved babies away to boarding school. But she liked knowing her paintings were safe and sound in a fine barn in Daylesford. Mrs Hamlin had promised to try to sell some of them, which would not be easy; Clarice could have done with the money, though, for supplies.

The shed would never be left unlocked again.

She resumed:

Mum is steadily frailer and hardly goes out anymore. One of the last times, incredibly, was three years ago, when we went to see Anna Pavlova and her company. The tickets were a treat from Father for Mum's birthday. Pavlova was an inspiration to me. I'm nervous to describe her, lest I dispel the magic with pedestrian words. Let me venture that she was equally sparkling and sombre, a silver apparition somewhere between sunshine and moonshine but within a live body absolutely athletic and refined, sensual and spiritual. There. I'll stop before making myself any more ridiculous. The evening was a throwback to the more stylish life we used to lead, when there was more money for cultural outings. It was really quite an idyll: Mum and me watching as if our lives depended on it, me manically sketching. I later tried a couple of little studies of my dancing idol, wispy things—total lightness being the only possible approach. There is no equalling her, of course. I could only fail miserably.

Louise has not had an easy time of it. The marriage soured. Both of them may have been a little too fond of drink and of having their own way. And I wouldn't be surprised if Ted had behaved vilely. L is now living alone with the kiddies, as we still call them, though her boys are turning into young men. The youngest, Charlie, has been problematic, rather taking after his father, I gather. L comes infrequently to the house, so we hardly see one another, except, very rarely, for a picture in town.

They had gone to see *Spite Marriage* and laughed side-splittingly at Buster Keaton's heartbroken face.

Leaving the theatre, Clarice said, 'The wayward girl's wicked deed is put right.'

'Quite. A nice fairytale. Keaton is awfully handsome.'

Clarice agreed. He made continual humiliation hilarious, but there was a sorrowful shadow about him or in his dark, dark eyes. It seemed that light could not stick to him, though his yearning for it could hardly be borne.

'That scene where he's trying to get his wife onto the bed!'

The shapes that floppy, stone drunk girl got folded into, and all those times she fell. It had been very intimate to watch that, like spying on an unimagined, subtle violence. But a different sequence was playing itself out in Clarice's mind. The married couple is alone on a ship at sea. The wife asleep, unknowing; Keaton, her husband, who masqueraded as a gentleman and has inadvertently become a sailor, finds himself in the engine room. He is up to his chest in water. All he can do is take the small bucket on hand, fill it, hurry like a trained monkey up the stairs onto the deck and empty it over the side. And back down the stairs. And over and over. All through the night, this endless, minute unseen work with the bucket to stop the boat from going down.

'Was it supposed to represent marriage?' she asked. 'The part on the boat with the bucket?'

'Hmm? Oh.' Louise chortled. 'Maybe. Rather accurate, in my experience.' She was quiet, then said, 'I think in many marriages someone uses a bucket and someone sleeps.' A few moments later, she added, 'It can be hard to tell the difference between floating and sinking.'

Clarice was sad for Louise, who had not got what she had anticipated from her destiny. And she did not have art or, say, religion to sustain her—a powerful distraction. Clarice sometimes felt as if Louise had thrown her to the wolves by leaving home to marry, but this was completely absurd.

It was a rare opportunity to be tender, and all she managed was, 'He wasn't good enough for you.' Though it sounded vacuous, she had meant it.

Louise said, 'Who would you want to play you, if they made a picture about your life?'

Clarice had never considered it.

'I'd choose Louise Brooks, my namesake. It's funny. Everyone says we look so much alike.'

I've kept to one solo exhibition per year at the Athenaeum and it is no trouble to produce this quantity of work. I'm not so scared of openings as I used to be. There is always the last frantic arduous night of hanging—the running around in a flap, shifting something, extracting a piece and adding another. I find it satisfying, and when the moment of reckoning comes and I'm standing there in a group of well-wishers in my Sunday best, I'm less uncomfortable in the limelight than you might think. Not that I relish the role, but I try to rise to the occasion and thank people and smile enigmatically, even if I am unslept and red-faced from childish bashfulness and wine. I have remained largely a teetotaller, so the latter goes to my head. The last show did not go badly, I suppose. A couple of critics came, but the crowd consisted mainly of old friends, Meldrum's cohort and admirers, plus the inevitable uppish stranger come to look down on me. Few purchases—nothing new there. Mrs H, the dear woman, bought several.

Mrs Hamlin had indeed outdone herself: crimson lipstick striking the senses first, then a powdered phosphorescence, veiled hat and formidable silk gown baring a long, abundant white back. Desperately wanting to be ravishing, she was.

She is her own work of art and I appreciate her more and more. Meldrum was there too, recently back from America, and quietly supportive. He said he was thinking of writing a second book on his theories. Though he was missing some of the usual vitality. He insisted I pay him a visit at Olinda. It had been ages—years—since we'd talked art. I have been remiss, out of touch with everyone, really.

I was true to my word and took the train to Belgrave, where he came for me by car. It's a lovely, bucolic place they have.

Meldrum had still seemed lacking in verve, a tad doleful, diminished, even in that peaceful setting. She noticed a little more grey in his beard, but nonetheless he recovered his energy and his step was lithe as he prowled the studio, presenting his recent work to her. He really was a skilled showman. Without quite wanting to reveal it, he appeared anxious for her response, almost as if he considered her his equal. She had not been his student for so many years, but now it was final. She had wondered if such a day would come and now that it had, her limbs were heavy; she was listless, somehow.

What to say? The work was, of course, technically irreproachable. And she had a soft spot for his fields, gums and dappled light, the resolute simplicity of his subjects.

However, there was something rigid or limited in what she saw. It hurt her to notice it, as it had hurt, as a child, to observe the limitations of Mum's watercolours. She could have been wrong, but she sensed in Meldrum's new work, more than anything, his self-discipline like a hard fist. She could not breathe deeply, looking at it; her mind was corralled.

'Masterful,' she said.

It occurred to her that he might set so steadfastly about depicting just what the eye could see (the innocent eye) that he forced himself to look through too small an objective and so forgot the edges of his vision. Out of his hatred for sentiment and storytelling, could he have gone too far, stripping away also feeling and suggestion? These, she had come to believe, were inseparable from sight, if not wound up in its very heart. How innocent was the eye, finally? The artist tried to be honest and clear-visioned, but remained human— an individual, with the sensitivities of his own gaze.

M is terrifically loyal to me. He was disgusted, he said, with the critics for their treatment of me, partly blaming himself for the attacks, so similar to those that plague him and all his 'followers' (uninspiring, mundane, dull, et cetera). He is depressed by Australian and particularly Melbourne parochialism, though Europe, easily seduced by ephemeral fashions, suffers from its own evils, in his opinion. He'd come across one generous review of my show, however, and read it to me. I've kept the clipping. There is a part of it that touches me, to the effect that some of my paintings give the viewer an impression of looking through an opening. Forgive me for mentioning this. I pretend to be indifferent to critics and at times I really couldn't care less, or laugh rather contemptuously about them. But I confess that in weaker moments I'm quite undone, so when there is a little bit of honey, it's hard to stop it from going to my head, like the wine I'm not used to drinking. One bolsters oneself as one can.

I remember our sunrise sessions and morning bathes with affectionate nostalgia. Were we children, then, in a way? Your circle must be fun and I'm glad they're appreciating you, as they should. Myself, I have no real coterie at present and have pretty much lost my hand at socialising—or don't need it. You'd call me a hermit, only I'm always out on the streets. Hardly seclusion.

You say that the girl is too young and you are not yet tempted to settle down. I understand you. Oh, dear: look at all these sheets. What a ramble! Paint up a storm. Catch that mellow, golden light.

Fondly,

Clarice

She was surprised to see this flood of words emerge from the intense quiet of her days.

23

The doors and windows were kept firmly shut, only at night letting in the thin breeze. Against this background of torpid summer heat that had them dozy and short-tempered, they toasted subduedly with their teacups to the new year of nineteen thirty-four.

After some clotted days spent in bed or else dozing in her chair by the window, Mum abruptly became wakeful and alert. At all hours, unpredictably, she could be found wandering through the house's stale rooms, her floral nightgown shifting softly against her loose flesh, a waft of L'Heure Bleue lingering after her. She had painstakingly preserved that bottle of perfume and the alcohol in the scent had begun to move forward, a hint of fermentation there; its intense powdery sweetness had formerly seemed excessive, headachy to Clarice, but now it was dulled and forlorn. The ageing perfume was eloquent: those last years of the tightening purse—no maids, so little entertaining and few excursions—had been hard on Mum.

Of course, she knew the house like she knew the inside of her own mind, but she now navigated it tentatively. She touched objects, a table, a dresser, a red curtain, as if they were hypotheses she was testing. Clarice followed her on these experimental walks, hovering a few steps behind and watching as unobtrusively as she could in the hope of catching a clue. Was Mum taking her bearings by those familiar landmarks? Or conducting some late inventory? Clarice breathed the close air threaded with murky old perfume, pining for transparent smells, ocean wind and the pungent sweat of eucalyptus leaves.

Very late one night, hearing Mum up, Clarice climbed out of bed and went to find her. She was in the drawing room, where the moon showed the opening arms of the mantelpiece clock paused at three. Her hand descended cautiously over a lamp. Just when it appeared she would touch the lamp, her hand grew nervous; it soared up, then plummeted. Mum's stance, arms hanging slackly, suggested she was absorbed by something more primitive than thought. She swayed on her feet, about to fall.

Clarice rushed forward; was this like a mother's worry? But the old woman had regained her balance.

'Hannah! Where's Hannah?' Father called from their room, groggy and imperious.

Mum turned. Her face did not recognise her husband's voice. There was no bewilderment in it. Just, perhaps, a certain irony. Plump, cherubic, Mum's face said, *I'm going along with appearances for now. But I see what this is. I see right through it.*

165

With Mum now obeying an arcane set of rules, Clarice began to go to the city less often. She did not regret this; maybe she had finally sated the hunger that used to drive her there. She would concentrate on the sea, for a time at least. But before she did, there was one other subject she wanted to paint. A railway station.

The platform's black awning was interrupted by a vertical rectangle filled with orange-yellow lines that hinted at departures and arrivals. White parallel lines were train tracks. A red signal light gleamed darkly from the top of a black pole. Other black poles rose into the air, several pairs joined near the top by cross beams, like a strange, unfinished edifice waiting for its roof. The poles became dimmer as they retreated towards the horizon through a pale blue haze. Pinkish blobs of light shone through this haze, and above it sat a secretive creamy sky.

There was no train in sight. No travellers. The place was deserted, an empty stage. No one going anywhere. There was just the possibility of travel, the idea of coming and going, a pure dream of movement in which everything was still.

The soft colours and edges could have been the result of tears in the viewer's eyes. Tears of the one left behind? Or traveller's tears?

In the house at Beaumaris they waited for the heat to give, but it did not, continuing merciless, somnolent, and Mum settled once more in her bed; she was a little pale now and often short of breath. She read novels, with great focus. Clarice and Father spoke laconically of meals and the invisible progress of the weather. It was an inward time of hushed voices and solemn footsteps. Mrs Murphy from across the street had her husband bring them groceries regularly; the Murphys were of a type that knows how to behave, dependably and almost imperceptibly, in a crisis.

Dr Broadbent dropped in to see Mum every couple of weeks. Then each week. The two conferred in private, like conspirators or lovers, Mum seeming to derive a somehow voluptuous pleasure from his visits. Clarice was not told what had been discussed, and did not ask. There was a new air of vulnerability in the house—of anticipation. Still, Mum did not give the impression of being out of spirits, not more than usual. She was eating small servings, but particularly savoured apricot jam and peanut biscuits, whatever had sugar in it or the aura of a treat. She was peaceful: if anything, only a touch more self-important than before, enjoying her laziness, tending towards smugness after Dr Broadbent had been around.

Clarice realised that she herself had a case of the doldrums. It was not being able to get away to paint. One aimless afternoon, she looked up *doldrums* in the dictionary and was relieved to discover among its meanings: 'certain parts of the ocean near the equator that abound in calms, squalls, and light baffling winds'. It cheered her to have this oceanic panorama to set against what she was experiencing; she rolled the word around in her mouth, envisioning flat but easily ruffled waves.

It was sometimes possible to pass the awkward edge of sleep by entering, through her mind's eye, one of her own landscapes, its forms more and more gentle until it had become a window into dreaming.

She had given Mum a sponge bath, got a fresh nightie on her, combed her thin but springy hair and finally applied a parsimonious drop of the muted L'Heure Bleue to each crepe de Chine wrist. A languorous, heavy afternoon like many that had preceded it. There was a stretch of hours yet to traverse before it would be time to get the supper on. Clarice thought of slipping out with her trolley for a while, but she had to be here, at hand.

Folding a damp washcloth, she said, 'Pot of tea?'

With a tone that did not seem insensitive, Mum asked, 'What news of your artist friends?'

'Ada? She was well, last I heard.'

'The Meldrumites.' Mum smiled. 'The mud-slingers—wasn't that the term?'

So Mum had read some reviews. 'It was, indeed. I had a note from Mr Meldrum recently. The group is having another artists' colony at Anglesea.'

'When's that, dear?'

'It starts next week, I think.'

'And you're going?'

'Oh, no.'

'You don't want to?' An implacable look in the faded dusky green of Mum's eyes.

'They've invited me—they always do. But I said no, of course.'

'Tea would be just what the doctor ordered. Just the thing. I'm parched.'

When Clarice came back carrying the tray, Mum turned from the window, a cushiony mass amid the frilly pillows of her bed. 'You'll go,' she declared, with the peculiar, daunting determination of the infirm.

Mum had begun to remind Clarice of Herb, before he left—she seemed to have the same steady assurance that there were good things in store for her. They had become curiously close, in a way, she and Mum, and it was not just the intimacy that physical dependence creates. Clarice had fantasised about escaping the house, longing for the richly ventilated present that was unfolding beyond the sickroom, as if on another temporal plane. But she did not think, now that an opportunity had been presented to her, that she could spend a fortnight away. It was more than a decade since she had gone to Anglesea and she would not even have considered going again were Mum not vehement, decided, apparently, on using her last sizeable strength to give Clarice some liberty.

Go, she breathed tensely, almost a moan.

It felt like love. And rejection.

The packing, the parting and the quick leaving were hideous. She arrived at Anglesea only to find that Father had telegraphed for her immediate return. She did not paint a single board there or even walk down to the place where the estuary flowed, at regular intervals, into the sea.

24

Though she had long thought of her mother as sickly, it was deeply implausible there could ever be an end to the continuum of her, yet here Clarice saw the plain evidence of a life concluding. She returned that same day from Anglesea to find that Mum's skin appeared to be petrifying and her smell was changing, less powdery now, sweetening into a strangely universal scent. In some barely conscious state, Mum did not open her eyes nor speak.

Clarice had known to expect something like this, eventually, but she was dumbfounded. What was happening was not only implausible; it was unacceptable, unnatural. Aberrant. It had to be stopped. She felt Mum's tepid forehead; she fussed with the already straight sheet. She stood, immobile, by the bed. There was nothing to do. What was her role? She retreated to a chair in the corner of the room, confused by her own helplessness. She watched, for hours. Others came and went by the bed. Father. Louise. Mrs Murphy. Battling to breathe, Mum's lips were bluish, bluer. Perhaps death and the end of the love act had this in common: the sensations experienced could not be fully shared; the dominant feeling at both times might be loneliness.

Sometime during the night, contemplating the slight significant shapes of the familiar body beneath the sheet, Clarice thought: she was my first seascape, the interior sea, a bone shoreline curving like a half moon. Floating in her, in the forgetful twilight before birth, I prepared for the waters of Port Phillip Bay. There, I was taught to seek nourishment curled in on myself. There, I first saw the feeling that haunts a shadow or a splotch of light; I knew her moods as dark washes or orange-red flashes against my unborn eyes, and my parents' affection for each other, perhaps, as a dull opalescence. Then, it was all incomprehensible and accepted.

At another indeterminate point, Louise touched Clarice's arm and said, 'You need to sleep.'

She studied her younger sister briefly. Louise's eyes were as she had never seen them, slow and deep, beautiful with mourning. 'I'm alright. Not tired, really.' Grazing the hand on her arm, she added, 'You go and rest.' Perfumed air. 'Wait.' Clarice took Louise's wrist and laid her nose to it, like a bloodhound; the old L'Heure Bleue, powdery and heartbroken. Delicately, she kissed that pale perfumed skin.

When the dawn came, she was remembering the watercolours that had hung in her parents' bedroom, especially the bird of paradise. She was calmer. In the deep shadow edged with pink, her mother appeared to be wearing a faint smile. She went over to the bed to see it better. It certainly resembled a smile. Contentment? Detachment?

Back in her chair, she sat up straighter. Her role, if not to share or understand, was to watch. It was always the way. I am your witness. This was far from passive; the effort required, the participation were devastating. Still not a lot to offer, but maybe a kind of gift.

Soon there was no expression on her face at all. Mum let go of her hold on the physical world and there was a shifting inwards, the vessel that housed her hinting heavily at absence. Then suddenly, quite clearly, starkly, the vessel was uninhabited; its tenant had moved on. She had departed this life.

Astonishing. Remarkable—this. So *large*. Clarice closed her eyes; she only half knew herself.

The house was warm and quiet, though there were more in it than normal. A relaxed Anglican, even in her distant days of singing in the church choir, Mum had not expressed an interest in seeing a priest; but Dr Broadbent had been called an hour earlier, when her breathing became more agitated and wispy. He now said, 'She's at rest.' Turning to Father and exhaling heavily, 'I'm sorry for your loss.' Glancing at Clarice and Louise, 'It's good to know she's finally at peace. I'll leave you all alone with her. Don't worry—I'll see to . . . things.'

'Thank you,' Louise said, uncertainly giving him her hand. He smiled.

'I'm going out to get some air. And to stretch my legs,' Father said. His face was as impassive as it had been all night, but he walked off with an unusual torpor.

'I'll go and help Mrs Murphy with the tea,' Louise murmured. Her steps travelled in the direction opposite to that of the kitchen; she was probably going to smoke in secret and to cry.

Nothing had changed since the last time Clarice looked at Mum's face: only the trace of an opaque smile from which it was impossible to pinpoint a mood. Her skin was cooling frighteningly fast; time, having been distended and unrecognisable, was reasserting a tight rhythm.

The stopped heart. Mum's weak heart.

Clarice put a hand over her own, presumed similarly weak, the weakness predetermined. There was its light thump, a little jittery with fatigue, but reliable. She would have known were her heart weak, would she not?

She had an odd sense of family. She saw each of them in turn. Father, making a careful lap of the garden. Louise, surreptitiously sucking at a cigarette, as seductive as a film star. Herself, hand over her stunned heart, in the smoky morning light. And their deceased: the young Paul, constructing himself a good foolproof noose; Mum, not as she had been in that bed but lifting a spoon of apricot jam to her waiting lips. Maybe they all shared, in their own fashion, unlikely resilience.

Pink flowers in a cut glass vase on the bedside table. What flower was that? The blooms had a somewhat artificial appearance. Clarice was not sure how they had got there. One of the Murphys must have brought them or else Louise, or Dr Broadbent, as a token from his wife. She had never been inspired to learn the names of flowers. Names—why? These had not wilted, despite the heat. In fact, when she inspected them, she discovered that the petals were firm and resistant, with something of the disconcerting upholstered feel of moths' wings. Touching them left her fingertips coated in a powdery residue, its scent surprisingly strong— too sweet, as if of some poisonous nectar. She lifted the flowers out of the vase; they dripped a ragged trail of water as she went to the kitchen.

Tea had been left out for her, but thankfully no one was there. She squinted at the flowers to grasp their mysterious forms, to comprehend how the yellow light touched them, where shadow adhered.

The unnatural flowers went into the garbage bin with a clean, sharp movement. Clarice rinsed the vase and her hands thoroughly, and inverted the vase to drain. Bending down, she removed her socks; it was important to have her feet naked against the jarrah floorboards, against the foundations of the house and the earth beneath. She carried her tea to the door, a bare foot pushing it open. Looking out, with eyes that had forgotten full light, she took a first swig of lukewarm tea.

And the grim and banal formalities of death ensued. When these too were behind them, the weeks became formless.

There was just painting, jumbled memories and Father's requirements to fill the time. As if there were a law by which there must always be illness in their home, Father's arthritic condition worsened. He took on a nurse to assist him, a rather difficult woman named Mrs Marks; maybe he was hoping to distract himself from Mum's desertion.

Clarice tried to envisage Mum in a realm of exquisite, unearthly light, such as that of a rainforest—or a beach at dusk, light like the surface of a pearl. She saw only a dark room with no windows in its walls. The room empty, unfurnished, dank.

There was not enough new work for her regular solo Athenaeum exhibition. Meldrum wrote urging her to visit again and to send some paintings for the coming group show. She wrote back saying she did not much feel like exhibiting, for the moment, but she was grateful for the offer.

Ada, strangely undaunted by Clarice's neglect and their stillborn friendship, showed herself to be an angel by sending a letter in which she suggested that Clarice go to stay with her family in the country. It came just in time, perhaps; with hindsight, Clarice realised there was not much good she could have done herself at home. Ada wrote lightly of *cheering up*, words becoming gossamer and limp close to death.

And Clarice received a second very great gift, from Mrs Hamlin. Fifty new panels, delivered by her son, who claimed they had been bought with the proceeds from the sale of a number of her paintings; he did not say which paintings or who had bought them. She had a surge of love for Mrs Hamlin, for her eagerness, her finery and her eager, fine heart.

By then, her supplies had dwindled to four canvases, three panels, little linseed oil and not a lot of paint. The bit of pocket money Father had used to give her each month, supplemented occasionally on Mum's urging, had not been forthcoming of late. She suspected there was no money to spare, not with the funeral expenses and Mrs Marks' salary. To preserve her precious materials, Clarice had taken to painting, with some blend of despair and amusement, on the backs of Wheaties packets: an appropriately flimsy, insubstantial experience.

After Mrs Hamlin's son had gone, she cried a little, holding the new panels. Tears, it seemed, were inexhaustible.

She had never particularly hankered for travel, except the kind that took her in a train to the city or in a motorcar to an art camp. She had not envied Herb or others for going abroad, to London or Paris, not really. There had always been plenty to keep her occupied, so much to overwhelm her where she was.

But she gave in to Ada because it was essential then that she get away. She saw no other way forward. She did not ask Father's permission, only informed him. There was a train ride and Ada's father came for her by car; she could not concentrate fully on the country she passed through. After, her recollection of that trip was a feeling of great age, slackness of mind and, when a window was opened, the wind as a cool surprise. At one stage, some grit had caught in her eye and it had taken a long time to dislodge it. Finally, they arrived at Naringal.

The Andersons, she discovered, were well-meaning people to whom, embarrassingly, she had absolutely nothing to give. They were an older couple but kept themselves fit, even athletic, maintaining their house and property on which they ran sheep and a few other animals for their own needs. Their four children (a fifth had perished in the Great War) were spread over three cities. Mr and Mrs Anderson seemed happy or unworried, eating large, quiet meals and going to bed early, always together. Clarice did not look forward to bedtime, to lying down—as if she fully expected to sleep—in the pose of a corpse.

The days at Naringal were a succession of cups of tea, sturdy china cups with perfect chains of roses around their rims. Clarice had little to say and was sure her company had to be a tiresome burden. Her sorrow was a stain in the Andersons' spotless, placid house; they showed no sign of noticing, however, and were gentleness itself. She did her best to eat the food they served, an overabundance of plain, nourishing stews and weekend roasts. Mrs Anderson thought Clarice's frame could use some fattening up. *Her* children were good eaters, the lot of them. The boys, in particular, had hollow legs, but even Ada enjoyed her meals, as Clarice would know. In fact, she knew nothing of their daughter's appetite and understood that the Andersons did not realise how negligible her knowledge of Ada actually was, not imagining that Clarice had avoided her supposed imitator, turned away from her as if from her own inconsequential shadow.

Cramped and moody with sleeplessness, she got up early with her hosts and stood a while after breakfast on the cold verandah, listening to the birds rouse the day. She was tender-headed, as dark and misty as the fields. She often feared she would not be able to keep down her porridge and would deposit the shameful, steaming contents of her stomach onto the admirable vegetable garden.

She was still Mum's daughter, there on the verandah so early in the morning you could have sworn it was night. She was the daughter of an emptiness, of emptiness—somehow even more a daughter now. It was strange how much love for a parent could feel like a wound. She clenched her teacup in her unfeeling hands and waited for a smudge of light.

Clarice was her own mistress, the entire day at her disposal, but she stuck to the old pattern, going out mornings and evenings.

Her preference was for empty paddocks with an especially bare look. It hurt a little to walk; she was out of condition, and her joints were not what they had been, her body officially no longer a girl's. Once, for a second, she thought she saw Arthur. That box of guilt had long been empty. At the far, right-hand margin of her sight, he stood watching her, smoking a meditative cigarette.

She was a ghost too, at first—she was painting like a ghost. Out of habit, without precision or wonder. She was like a priest deserted by his faith, who nonetheless continues to go through the motions, getting up at dawn to the ritual of prayer, as much a part of him as that of breathing. She saw that self-hatred played no small part in devotion. The discomfort of her body, stiffly shaped to her will, was gratifying. Points of pain tingled in her arms. Tightness bound her wrists. Fatigue ignited a slow fire in her back. When she swayed on her feet from long concentration, she steadied herself with her easel, one hand clenched around the mast. She was pleased, on the verge of collapse.

It took many days to see the place, to make sense of it. Close to the end of her stay, it dawned on Clarice that the tea she drank continually at Naringal was strong and golden-glossy with the decadent cream of farm milk. Around this time, she stopped reusing her panels, painting heartlessly over scenes she had already painted.

Her mind and soul in the mud, a moment had finally come in which she knew, truly understood she was a painter. Painting did not matter anymore. Nothing mattered but painting. This was all there was. And there was nothing to achieve. The paintings might be seen by few, might go unseen. So be it. They were enough unto themselves.

Painting in the void. What made a day intelligible was the donkey work of teasing something into being in tone and form where there had been a blank. She could do anything she wanted with paint, anything. She could fail and succeed, suffer uncertainty, but all of that would be beside the point. Everything was permitted and possible. She felt the weight of her vocation. The startling freedom of it. She was born to this. No Clarice outside painting; she was Clarice because she was a painter and she was a painter because she was Clarice.

In twenty-one days, she completed two canvases and thirty panels. She enjoyed working on board, the smooth flatness of paint gliding onto wood, without the drag that

179

canvas imposed on the brush. She kept the work quick and fluid, unmediated by thought, as far as it was possible: physical. Paintings of Naringal paddocks. In some the sun was smaller, and in others, larger, fuller. There were more or fewer trees. The trees were far or close. Sometimes, fence posts could be discerned in the distance. Or the grasses appeared to undulate. It amused her to give the scenes names. There was one she called *The three trees* in homage to Meldrum, to his brave work of perhaps two decades earlier. Many were informatively entitled *Fields*, *Landscape*, *Summer Landscape* or some such thing. The Andersons went to great pains to be complimentary, and even bought several, but found them, Clarice could see, perplexingly monotonous and drab. She was surprised to note her eyes going to their faces to find approval—the old reflex.

Just as her self was annihilated and definitively fused to painting, Clarice re-emerged. She became a woman again, of blood and impulses; she had confident hips and strengthening thighs, greater mental elasticity. It was being out in the open, day after day, in the new place. It was the wind stroking those dry grasses, the unstoppable rolling of the sky. It was the aching of her arms and the endless, conquering renewal of change.

One morning as she was finishing up, she tipped her head back and her hat fell off. The breeze teased the sweat on her forehead. Her head was so far back that there was a slight pain in her throat and her legs folded. She was sitting in the middle of the paddock. She pried the palette and brushes from the fist of her left hand. The rough grass tickled through her stockings.

Those desiccated fields were the colour—the *exact* colour—of the sand of certain beaches she knew intimately. The name of the colour was on her tongue. *Gamboge.* So came the revelation confirming what for some time she had dimly sensed. The grass she was looking at was a veneer, which, scratched away, revealed itself to be sand; while sand, if approached correctly, could no doubt be similarly peeled back to expose the underlying grass.

It was all fashioned of the same matter. Each landscape was far deeper than itself—yet indivisible, one.

When she was finished with the fields, when she went home, she would paint Port Phillip Bay as it had not previously been painted. Indeed, her paintings would not resemble any others; they would be the whole truth of what she saw.

Retrieving her hat, she whimsically decided that she would also try putting a man in a landscape, as an experiment, to see what would happen. In the meantime, mornings and evenings she checked her kit was in order and set out for work, recommencing the occult, triangular conversation, stepping into the circle made by artist, paint, subject. She was a grateful labourer.

25

Her hands were always thinking and ready, a pulse of energy tapping at her fingertips. She slept little and sporadically. It was not like the insomnia she had known at other times; there was none of that dread of the next day feeling squishy and afflicted, like spoiled fruit. Her body was simply loath to waste the hours set aside for rest, preferring to lie in bed vigilant, crisscrossed by bright, flitting ideas, priming itself for the dawn. Sometimes, she read—joyful Whitman, treatises on theosophy, mysteries, anything she happened across.

Things were as different after Naringal as she had imagined they would be that day in the field when her hat fell off from staring at the sky. She achieved the vantage point that made homemaking routines fences within which she could run. She was no domestic angel; books lay open and splattered on the kitchen bench and her matted hair hung in front of her eyes as she peered erratically into steaming pots, her cooking giving queer results. But Father, oddly, did not often complain. There was more space for her mind, her artist's mind, a liveliness cutting through anything tedious and soul deadening. She was stronger, harder-headed or higher-spirited than ever before. She ate with appetite again, if not plentifully, her principal hunger not being for food. She got very thin, turning into some strange sister to the whip of a girl she had once been.

Conscious that the senses of a good woman were supposed to be dull and incurious, Clarice had sometimes in the past tried to bar the gate on hers, hyperactive as they were— invariably a vain enterprise. Now she allowed herself to receive the infinitude of sensations offered with an accepting heart. She often hummed Debussy, that slyly delightful music she had not heard in an age.

She did what she could to avoid Father's nurse, who visited every day and seemed to relish being omnipresent. If Clarice was lingering quietly in a room, Mrs Marks infallibly made it her business to enter that room on an obscure mission. Sternly, the nurse advanced, with a slight forward tilt, as if determinedly crossing the deck of a ship on a troubled sea. If Clarice rushed in from work in a flap, wild-haired and stinking of turps, Mrs Marks was waiting; her nose twitched and her gelid, censorious gaze perused the intruder, whom she obviously judged sorely lacking in daughterly virtue. At these moments, Mrs Marks made unilluminating yet dour pronouncements of the kind: 'What your father *really* needs is rest.' Clarice appeared to represent an obstacle to this rest. She would limit herself to a faintly ironic 'yes indeed,' or a 'quite'. Mrs Marks was not interested in talking, though. Her lips remained tight with disdain. Clarice saw the word *eccentric* pass through the nurse's appalled mind, trailing a freight of sauciness and depravity.

However, if Mrs Marks got on her nerves, Clarice was now more at ease with Father. His uncompromising nature had, if such a thing were possible, been distilled. But there was also a wavering quality to him that had not been quite visible before. And his gruffness was almost like some prickly old friend. She realised that his voice no longer echoed in her head. Not needing to make a fortress of herself, she could be generous with him. He wanted her at home, assuring him unmolested quiet; she was, during the times of the day when his need for her was most acute.

She hardly saw or heard from Louise, indeed she saw no one, really, outside the domestic sphere. Almost no one.

Though they had glimpsed one another by the bay more days than not for some twenty years, Clarice had waved only once or twice to the man she thought of as the Doctor. They knew one another purely by sight, but she felt they were curiously connected, as fellow worshippers of the religion of daily walking. She was planning to address him.

He had a stately and composed bearing, appearing closed inside the enjoyment of his exercise; she liked to infer that the outdoors was sacred to him. His stride was leisurely or patient, not without ambition but having nothing to prove. The evening hour was his favourite. And hers. Morning was an instinctual communion with nature. Evening was mature introspection, maybe philosophy. She thought he was an evening creature.

From rumour filtered through Mum, she had learned his specialisation—cardiology—and in which street he lived behind which façade, and that he had a quite successful clinic in East Melbourne. His wife, who was ailing, was almost never seen by anybody, but on Sundays he regularly took his two girls on an outing into the city. The girls had recently come out and were much admired, both reputed to be charmingly lovely, though one, Clarice gathered, tended to be fretful and the other a bit flighty. She imagined the Doctor was a doting father, to a fault.

A good deal of space had always separated them. One evening, she eliminated it.

'Hello. We're always passing one another, aren't we?'

He accepted the greeting as she had thought he might, unstartled.

'What is that you push around?' he asked with a certain inevitability.

'This? This is my painting studio. You haven't ever seen me working?'

He paused. 'Of course. How couldn't I? The lady landscape painter.'

'The batty bluestocking?' How odd that after a long silence there was suddenly this flow of words linking them.

'On the contrary—you're thought of as a talent. They say you exhibit.'

'I've had my moments,' she said a little archly, studying the back of her not-very-dainty freckled hand.

'You're a local legend,' he continued, and now in his voice there was something subtly reckless. Their faces did not change; they seemed to have known the conversation would take this turn, becoming private. 'They say you keep to yourself.'

'Ah? Do you call this keeping to myself?'

He smiled. In the distance, a small dog frisked into view.

'I've very often seen you painting. You seem so absorbed. I was curious about that.' He lifted his walking stick and pointed again at her cart.

'Yes, well. It holds my kit. I made it myself.'

'Really?' A faint amusement, but no surprise.

She did and did not want to be the topic of conversation. 'And you're a doctor, who likes to walk.'

With convivial self-mockery, he said, 'My constitutionals.'

She observed that he chose to be enhanced rather than diminished by his years; he had an air of dignity, but he played the part of the conservative elderly doctor—it was a performance he was accustomed to, though able to drop.

'Now we're friends, maybe you'll show me one of your paintings, some time?'

She stood ramrod straight. 'I'll do better than that. I've been wondering if I might paint your portrait.'

The Doctor looked at her quickly, obliquely. Then his gaze travelled to some point on the sea.

'Please assure me,' he said in a soft voice, 'you don't paint from the nude.'

She had a troublesome sprightly feeling and laughed flatly to create a smokescreen around it. 'Not generally. We're not in Montmartre.'

'Indeed, we're not,' he said, looking at her again. 'I'm comforted.' His head was tilted, his chin a little lifted. 'Flattered. But I'm not sure I'd be a very good subject.'

'I didn't have a traditional portrait in mind. It'd be done in the open. I'd set you against a landscape.' She added, 'It would be very masculine.'

'You're poking fun at me. Which is disrespectful. Haven't you been taught to respect your elders?'

'Yes, but I'm not all that good at obedience.' Had she expected this would be so light and fast? The wind off the sea was powerfully perfumed, mild.

'Do you paint at home too?' he asked. 'Or just out here?'

'A little at home . . .' She hesitated. 'In the kitchen, at night.' She watched his eyes stealthily; he was paying attention, she thought. 'I've envied other artists—men, really—their studios. But I've had this, haven't I?' So much talk, and it felt unnaturally honest. 'If I were reincarnated and had to choose between this and a different artist's life, I'd probably wind up with my exact same fate again.' She chuckled. 'I'd be back here over and over, pushing this silly old beast around.'

'Old beast,' he repeated, appearing to like this. 'Do you believe in reincarnation, then?'

'I'm coming to think I believe in most things.'

The Doctor's eyes were direct and speculative. Clarice realised that they had not introduced themselves, as if they were already too familiar with one another to bother. They took the steps, half-solemnly, that this dance required. And while they waited for him to agree to entrust himself to her brush, the night laid itself slowly out for inspection.

26

Because it was so difficult, Clarice painted the Doctor twice, the second painting following the first with hardly a pause, just the time to get him settled in the new position and for her to half-heartedly clean her brushes with a rag. The paintings were a surprise and at the same time confirmed something.

He was not at all sedate, in paint. A thickset man in his early sixties, he was distracting; you would have to say ominous. He threw you off balance, seeming more a tenebrous night bird than a human being. Given the choice, you would surely not trust him. He stood in nature in her paintings, but he was unmistakably the star of the show.

The colour in the first was lurid by her standards, brash, with slathers of biting yellow-green, and the man leaned against the railing of a small white bridge. He was appraising the viewer—possessively, arrogantly?—from under the brim of his hat. A cane hung from his arm. He had something but not everything of the grumpy old man. His eyes were a dark band across a face in which just the tip of his nose and his mouth emerged into light. And the darkness deepened as your eye journeyed over his figure. One arm and most of his torso were virtually black, the black continuing down to his thighs, where it abruptly stopped—making him appear an amputee, miraculously standing on the memory of legs.

For the second painting, she had positioned him at the end of a pathway bordered by trees. The trees' shadows fell across the path and he too was a shadow, a gloomy form, whose ponderousness was relieved only by the slight blue filigree of ocean discernible through the trees over his left shoulder. This glimpse of water gave the impression of serving as some kind of laughable talisman or prayer.

She had hoped he would be a complicated subject and she had sweated as she worked, but Clarice was certain of the extent of the challenge only when she saw him on her panel, remade in light and shade. She shivered, thinking that perhaps you could confide things, dark things, to the man in these paintings without shocking him; or the dark things would not need to be spoken, they would just sit, almost calmly, between the two of you.

'I'm uglier than you expected?' He was quick.

'No. You're magnificent.' He was.

She had not tried to pin a character to a board since the early, green portraits. To attempt it was always arrogance: at best, you got only a sliver of your subject into paint. If you were lucky, however, the sliver turned out to be raw—it came from the quick. And perhaps she had finally come close to luck, with the Doctor; too soon to tell. Not quite sure what to make of these new works, she thought she might like to continue painting people—him, at least—investigating further. Clarice wanted more of this thrilling cocktail of power and subservience. His shoulders sagged once she was finished and he turned deferential, hollowed. But she did not think he was unhappy.

He would not be persuaded in for a bathe, despite the closeness between them, such that forms between model and artist, a mysterious reciprocal knowledge not born of language. From the water, she watched him reclining on the sand. It was a day of rare, loose freedom reminiscent of Anglesea. She savoured her own buoyancy and primitive mistrust of the waves; here, on occasion, even strong swimmers had been carried out to the depths.

She had told Father she was meeting Ada, the old pretext, and had no idea how the Doctor had achieved his day's leisure. They were twitchy when they met, secrecy always heightening an atmosphere. Not long after she began work, they both stilled.

She waved to him on the beach and he did not wave back; his eyes might have been closed. His appreciation of the outdoors, she was learning, did not involve admiring views or geography. He praised fresh air for its healthful properties, believing it generated fortitude and oiled thinking. She was fascinated by this, by his not living through his eyes.

It seemed criminal that she had not swum in so long. Ocean swimming, soothing a tired, over-excited intellect, was the panacea for the artist's taxed brain. This was the effect of painting: it depleted her just as it left her with an excess of energy. She noticed that physically she wearied more quickly than she used to, though she was still able to stay out there till her breathing slowed, and her heart was strong, steady. Sky and sea were the two halves of the universe, the lower oddly flexible and varyingly opaque.

There were chaste times, when your ideas might be called *pure*. There were days when you were a saint, nothing fresher or neater than the inside of your mind, and days when you were rather wicked. Need was like this shifting ocean, now tormented, now quiet. As sure as it retreated, it would advance again. It seemed that, for better or worse, she found married men the more interesting or appealing. She was drawn to them. It may have been a coincidence. Or their married state suited her, allowing her to belong to herself. There could be deliciousness, of course, in prohibition and contravention; in frustration and covert happiness. Pain, too. She looked now in herself for guilt, something resembling the guilt she had felt with Arthur, and was relieved not to find it: she seemed to have surpassed that. And she was aware of none in the Doctor. The air between them was clear. Floating on her back for a moment, she thought, the history of one's lovers is somehow linked to the history of one's art. Both art and love are openness, the lowering of the walls that protect us from the world. Also true, perhaps, that art and love are forms of absurd hope in the face of tragedy and banality. Absurd or not, you continue hoping, try to hope convincingly, to open further.

She arrived at his feet dripping and silly-limbed.

His hat was over his eyes, his head resting on his folded jacket; he was probably dozing. She found even his sense of his own intelligence agreeable, as it did not prevent an interest in others. This might have had something to do with being a doctor, a servant of humankind.

She prodded his leg with her wet toe, feeling it tense.

'I'm off to get changed.'

She grabbed her things and turned her back on him quickly, wondering if he had taken the hat from his eyes to contemplate her very slender but forty-eight-year-old figure in bathing attire. How would he find her? There was no predicting what he would see.

It was a simple picnic of bread and cheese, some pickles she had taken a chance on with unusual success, an orange each and cordial to drink.

'We don't have any alcohol at home,' she apologised.

'Actually, I have some brandy.' He drew a flask out of the pocket of his jacket.

'Good,' she said. Then, 'Was it as traumatic as you expected?'

'Very, yes. It'll take me a while to recover. I guess I should gracefully accept that you can't have art without suffering.'

'You poor thing.'

'It's not very sporting to tease me. It was about time I was immortalised for posterity.'

She was happy that he entertained her. 'Don't you think you look distinguished?'

They studied the paintings that were drying, one against the cart and the other on her paint box, two additional members of their party—silent, possibly the more eloquent.

'A bit grim. Frightening, even. Do I really look like that?'

'I discovered that as I was painting.' She could not be sure that she had not intuited those things in him well before the first time they spoke. But she had *seen* that face by looking straight at it, squinting; it had been too late by then to avert her eyes, though she would not have missed it. The paintings were not peaceful depictions of a proud medical professional, an upstanding citizen and father. No.

Looking away from them and from his vague discomposure, she reached for the flask and took a molten sip. They were quiet.

As they were finishing their meal, the Doctor said, 'This has made me feel young. Can I prescribe myself this medicine again, Clarice?' He spent a moment fitting the lid to the cordial bottle and added, 'Will you want to paint me again or has the subject been exhausted?'

She pouted pensively, an expression she had seen on Louise. 'There's always more work to be done.'

'Glorious day.' He was jolly now. 'Despite my sufferings for art. You know, I have a huge respect for you bright, modern girls. Your generation. Faced with so many new ideas, the new times . . . I wonder about growing up hearing stories of the war and seeing men going off and not coming back. Or coming back in pieces.' He had turned sober, but rallied. 'And having so much more independence than your mothers did. Yours is a very different world.'

193

She took this to mean that their worlds, hers and his, were so entirely different as to be incompatible and it was a miracle they had come together at all. Maybe, too: Poor dear, you'll never marry. Though the compliment and the curiosity, she felt, were real. She was not displeased that he had spoken of her as a girl or that she baffled him.

27

She got more comfortable on her side, propping herself up on one elbow, and gazed at him from the shelter of her good hat. There was only a thin strip of bare sand between them. Other people are enigmas; he was miraculous. The food or the brandy had brought out the red in his lips. He was a lot older than Arthur and it showed, his body more solid, less supple. He was not so much paternal as avuncular, though, with something subtly debonair about him and a deadpan sort of humour. He reasoned deliberately, seeming to trust logic to clarify and resolve.

His face said he did not love her, not yet conclusively, or it preferred to remain unread; she was not at all bothered. Waiting for love was like waiting for a revelation. You had to be patient. And, on that glowing afternoon, she was pleased to consider herself not the marrying kind. An artist had to bring to the craft a free spirit, a spirit capable of falling in love continually with everything, everyone, and devoting itself to the daily labour of this love. How could such a woman's spirit sustain itself tethered by law, religion and duty to one man?

She took up his reference to the war: 'Were you a soldier?'

He made a rapid little gesture, adjusting his hat. 'As a doctor.' She did not expect he would talk about it and he did not. After a while, he continued, detached, 'We've all lost our innocence.'

'Were we innocent before?'

Brusquely, he leaned over and touched her arm.

She caught her breath and remarked, 'After painting, you feel terribly lazy. You turn into a sluggard who just wants to be waited on. You think how nice it would be to have a slave or two.'

'With palm fronds to fan you with and so on?'

'Exactly.'

His hand remained on her arm. The salt on her skin was a light, fizzy burning. She took the flask from him.

'We've almost finished it.'

In fact, there was only one mouthful left; she swallowed it.

'Would you know what it was to be waited on, if it came up and tapped you on the shoulder?' he asked.

'I'm very keen to learn. I'm sure I'd have considerable aptitude.'

'I imagine you would.'

He kissed her palm. His mouth was soft. Still cool from the water, her skin tightened into gooseflesh.

'What can this humble servant offer you, Madam?' he inquired croakily.

It was a good game. Perhaps it had been many years since he had known romance, but he had not lost the necessary vivacity, had not given up on its return. Nor had she.

'Oh, just leave me to sleep, won't you? Be gone.'

She stuck out her tongue and rolled onto her back. He waited a moment and then laughed, placing his hat over her face. She stayed beneath it, acquainting herself with the sweetly oily scent of his Brilliantined hair. When her lungs knew it, she passed the hat to him and the immense sky spread across her vision.

If desire were low, impure, then why did it feel holy, shooting up through the other layers till it broke free? Naturally, it entailed the risk of perdition, the undoing of the Family, and this was why it was ignored or shunned. Because it revealed many marriages as a lie or at least a half-truth. It was an ideal, a blindness, maybe even a sort of self-annihilation, and these things were dangerous.

Was then the powerful current of desire in the human a mistake, something the superior intellect of the *homo sapiens* should have overcome—but had not—during the evolution that brought him forward? Was it a kind of vestigial limb with no proper function? Yet there was the temptation to use the limb. Man lived with it uneasily, willing it invisible; nothing controlled you so forcefully as what was invisible.

'I think I'm drunk,' she said.

Her eyes swelling with the sky, Clarice wondered if the culmination of physical pleasure felt like a small death because it was a moment of grace in which the tragedy of life's end was shown to be beautiful. Yes, what if desire were not low, the sorry mess of corruption they would have you judge it, but rather the highest force, the lushest thing—not what religion was required to repress, but religion itself, the true face of God, the superbly ruthless machinery of existence?

'I get giddy,' she observed and, turning towards him, ordered, 'Come here.' Graciously, he obeyed.

In his disoriented surrendering, she caught a flicker of Meldrum, the day he properly noticed her. The Doctor and Meldrum were both Older Men and Important Persons, but until then she had not compared them. She acknowledged that they had in common a quality of being unusually substantial; without being touched, they were tangible. Arthur had been like that too, in his way, though she had learned to see his bravado, the masked desperation. The man beside her was more quietly, less gregariously attractive than either Arthur or Meldrum. To begin to feel it, you had to look at the Doctor side-on or paint his portrait.

28

They had been intimate for a number of weeks, and she had thought about it but always managed to stop herself in time—until she did not. She got the number from the operator and rang the Doctor's clinic. She put this illogical behaviour down to her interest in the other side of him, the illuminated side that others saw.

'Can I help you?'

Hearing the strained cordiality in his secretary's voice, Clarice took a dislike to her. Was it jealousy? Knowing she spent each day close to him?

'I wanted to make an appointment.'

'Yes. Can I ask the nature of the problem?'

She was momentarily stumped. There was no problem—or was there a problem? 'I need to see the doctor,' she got out.

'Could you be a little more specific?'

This struck her as impertinent and she replied, perhaps testily, 'It regards my heart.'

'The doctor *is* a cardiologist.'

It went without saying, of course, that her problem should be a matter of the heart. But still, there had been no need for sarcasm.

'Well, that's perfect then! Could you make an appointment for me, please? The name is Jane. Jane Young.' She enjoyed this banal alias, and the tingle it produced gave her an insight into why a person might want to run away, to be someone else. 'Shall I spell that for you?' she asked courteously.

For her shady excursion to East Melbourne, she wore a dark skirt and a white blouse. Hidden under her sleeve, a bracelet: a trinket Louise had given her one birthday, with exuberant bottle-green ovals of Czech glass.

In the waiting room, she tried to read a magazine. Her attention strayed.

At last, the secretary invited her to stand. A door was opened for her. And she was in his office.

The Doctor. At work. Decorous in his suit, serious, a touch tired, head to one side. She knew that angle of his head. He was sitting behind a mammoth desk; the desk was like his own island, or maybe a raft he was floating on.

He lifted his eyes. They reached her, saw—froze. He was good at dissembling surprise; something in his eyes recoiled, his face staying expressionless. She did not speak.

'Miss *Young*?' he asked, after a moment.

'That's right.'

A pause. 'What can I help you with?'

'Obviously, it's my heart,' she said, sheepishly.

He nodded. 'Obviously.' She was not sure if he was angry. 'Could you change into this smock, please? And we'll . . . have a listen.'

He stood and turned to the window. Apparently, it had started raining; she had not anticipated that. Perhaps he wanted to hypnotise himself, watching the rivulets against the pane.

She went behind the screen. Her elbow knocked it as she fumbled with her buttons.

'Remove everything on top, if you will. Including the brassiere.' He said this with absolute detachment.

Her blouse had caught on the bracelet. She battled with it, trying to free the fabric from the brass chain that pinched the skin of her arm. The blouse would not come free; her face was growing hot. He must have been able to hear she was having difficulties, but though he knew how to assist in her undressing, he did not come to help. With a desperate final tug, she liberated herself from the blouse, ruining it and not caring. A cluster of white threads hung from the bracelet.

She came out in the smock. He turned away from the rain's even inward light. It was gloomy in his office, and his face, beyond the small reach of the desk lamp, was saturnine. They considered one another.

Then he said, 'Right'—a trace of vengeance in his smooth tone?—and stepped towards her, holding a stethoscope. She lifted her chin.

His hands had not felt so cold before. He parted the smock and placed the frigid metal on her chest; knowing he was a witness to it, her heart raced. She avoided his eyes, after that.

He listened, saying nothing. She watched the whey-coloured window. Glad to have forgotten an umbrella, she craved the moment when she would be out in the rain, her clothes heavy and defiled by water. From out of the corner of her eye, she noticed that his hands were now empty; he had finished with the stethoscope.

But it was not over. He opened the smock once more and his fingers returned to her chest, to below her left breast, touching without tenderness. This method of palpation was absent, expert—gentle and cold.

'The heart can be felt through the body?' she asked.

His forehead was tight. 'It can.'

His fingers continued their purposeful work, raising the flesh of her breast out of their path, as if wanting to burrow between her ribs to something more tender and essential than bone. She had a painful urge to laugh. She glared at the veiled window, but there was nothing for it and she heard herself chuckle. He did not reciprocate her reprehensible mirth and made no attempt to put her at ease. She laughed more, dissolving, gasping. Perhaps she felt a pulse in his fingers—or was it hers? She overcame the laughter. In his attentive absent manner she recognised something, suddenly, from her own painting self. Ah. This was how an observer might look. So alert and dispassionate. He and she both knew how to be there and not there, this wonderful disappearing act.

He took his hands away and stored the stethoscope in a neat, slender case. That case might have held an expensive gift—a man's pacifying offering to his wife. It was over.

Soon after, to his secretary, he murmured, 'There will be no charge.'

They never spoke of the incident. That side of the Doctor did not talk to the side she knew. Or only rarely. Once or twice since, he had again felt her heart through a soft gap in her ribs, his fingers walking a tightrope between power and submission. Was he measuring his effect on her? Was there a warning in what he felt? Had he discovered a hereditary trap waiting to spring, or some other danger? He never told her what he learned; perhaps he was not able. She would have resisted the examination, squirmed away, only she was transfixed by his face. She had looked into it, as if finding herself with a looking glass, as honestly as she could.

FOUR
The Storm

29

She drifts the way a person considered dreamy drifts, afloat but vaguely aware of the censure of onlookers. At the Moira Private Hospital, the days have the confounding texture and aftertaste of dreams. Doctors and nurses labour to keep the patients enslaved to the laws of the material world with rites of nutrition and hygiene, social niceties, polite conventions, when all the while the edges of things are so indistinct, Clarice herself might have painted them. Quite often, she could swear she was standing behind her easel.

Today her chair has been wheeled into the solarium, where she is listening to a Chopin Nocturne. However, there is no sign of a gramophone and nor does anyone appear to be playing a piano. She checks the faces of the few other patients present; if they hear the music, it does not seem to affect them. But note surrenders to note. The Nocturne is shallow and limpid, dipping occasionally into obscure depths.

Since the storm, her thinking often takes an aquatic turn,

as though the drenching had soaked through to her brain. Her mind has become an ocean at low tide, the broad sands of the past exposed. She once attempted such a scene with a rather giddy palette—hot-hearted sunrise colours radiating from the vast mirror of a damp shore. She refused to let Arthur have the painting and he went sullen on her. To make him forgive her, she stroked her favourite part of his head, where his hair was receding. That night, he bit her lip; it could have been an accident, her mouth filling with slick, salty warmth.

The music continues, though no one heeds it but herself.

30

There is a vase of tight roses on the bedside table, not quite the pink of the flowers that accompanied Mum's passing. Father sits in the visitor's chair and of course the parasitic Mrs Marks is with him. Cut flowers fill Clarice with the same moroseness that zoo animals do. There is no light in Father's skin; he does not appear well.

'Louise was here,' he announces. 'You were asleep.'

A flaccid silence. When Clarice glances through the door into the hall, she sees a girl pass. The girl's name is Olive; she seems to remember someone introducing them. Olive wears too light a frock and she is twirling, arms spread wide. The zip at the side of the frock is open, offering a glimpse of pale body. She moves rapidly, unsteadily, but languorously too. Clarice is glad to have seen this. Soon after, Olive can be heard thumping into a wall, though she does not cry out.

'Heavens!' comments Mrs Marks. 'This place.' She stands fussily at Father's side, scowling with her purplish mouth.

The way she has of laying her hand on his back is distinctly proprietorial, wifely. What would Mum have thought?

'Clarice,' her father says, 'I warned you something like this would happen.' He mumbles, 'Going out painting in all weather. It was bound to happen.'

'Of course it was,' scolds Mrs Marks. 'Fancy getting caught out in the rain.'

A coughing fit helps to disguise Clarice's hilarity.

Father is repentant. 'When you get better,' he improvises, 'when you come home . . .' He fidgets in his chair, his knee probably hurting, a detail in a masterpiece of discomfort. 'You could paint some flowers.' He nods curtly at the roses he seems to have brought her and concludes, 'Those might inspire you.' The word *inspire* and the appeasing tone are foreign, unsettling for him.

'It's almost time for your lunch,' declaims Mrs Marks, speaking to Father. 'And'—her voice dropping to a whisper befitting a risqué confidence—'your medicine.'

Their conversations are always this airless and dreary. Clarice strains for a sound beyond the nurse's voice. She wishes Olive would come spinning back down the hall in her party frock. Who introduced them? Thankfully, after a while there is the lopsided noise of a person dragging a bad leg. Much of her entertainment here has been deciphering sounds.

'Your paintings of floral arrangements were pretty. They were nice.' Father is really extending himself. Perhaps he would not have made a bad art critic. She imagines him saying, *mawkish veils of fog*. 'The arthritis has been bothering me,' he adds.

210

He laces his fingers together, illustrating his unease. She thinks of a prestidigitator coolly displaying the result of a magic trick.

She squints and his fingers take on the fuzziness of distance. She tries to bring back Pavlova in *The Dying Swan*, struggling but finally drawing the ballerina into her mind's eye: effort so consummate and finely honed that it was erased; grace.

When she is indifferent enough to speak, she volunteers, to no one in particular, 'In my first solo exhibition, I hung one hundred and ten paintings in plain frames. I really prefer a plain frame.' Short sentences are easier. 'Eleven were still lifes of flowers. Only eleven of one hundred and ten—all the rest landscapes.' She does not cough, but when she breathes deeply, there is a little rattle. 'One hundred and ten minus eleven makes ninety-nine. Ninety-nine landscapes . . . One critic called his review *Flowers and Vases*.'

Coughing from another room, sharp and staccato. She is not the only cougher at the hospital; there is a choir of them. They each follow a different melody, but are made brothers by the same carnal beat.

She giggles. 'Can't anyone do arithmetic?'

Father and his nurse are looking perturbed. They find her incomprehensible. How long did it take Mrs Marks to perfect that inhuman look? Could she have been born with it? The two of them are not unlike art critics, secretly pleased to witness how landscape painting has overcome her; they are colourblind to her victory. Clarice's tolerance for talk has evaporated. She longs for her own nurse, a reassuring robust redhead, to come and drive them away, and is tempted to summon her with the bell. We each have a nurse now, Father, she thinks—how comical. The redhead has become her defence, the monarch of the country of her illness, just as Father is ruled by his hard-mouthed queen, Mrs Marks. Clarice must have become weak; she never required anyone's protection before. And yet she is feeling quite feisty.

'Father, go home and rest,' she tells him in a stranger's voice. The white ceiling hovers above her bed. 'You must be tired. Thank you for coming.' She makes small circles with her wrists beneath the wool blanket. 'And for the flowers.' Her chest is a little sore, but she rolls over till she is facing the door. 'Incidentally, I haven't painted flowers for a long time,' she says. 'And I have no plans to. Ever again. You should know that.'

The redhead, finally, as though wishing for her had caused her to materialise. She touches Clarice's forehead knowingly; it is like the cold, salty ocean on sun-provoked skin. Clarice wants more of that touch, wants sleep, her visitors gone.

The redhead leaves her frame of vision to speak to Father and his queen. Mrs Marks' voice is withering, the redhead's matter-of-fact, low, as she enunciates the queerly cushioned words *double pneumonia*. A twinge of alarm in Clarice's chest. She is missing the Doctor.

31

She is a prolific dreamer at the hospital. One night, or perhaps day—the line dividing these states is no longer quite fixable—Clarice is lying between two men in a rather grand four-poster bed. The bed has a canopy whose drapes seem to be filmy, restless pieces of the sky itself, a breeze lifting and subtly rearranging them. The sheets they lie on have an extraordinarily fine texture, impossibly smooth. As for the men, they are familiar, though she cannot definitively place them and they are therefore somewhat, but not altogether, menacing. The three of them are cocooned like triplets in the delectable sheets, floating drapes and balmy breeze. The sea is not far away.

She struggles to keep her thoughts in order, get things straight. Difficult to decide what she prefers: the never-ending circular caresses low on her back with the heel of a palm or the halting journey of a slightly ragged fingernail over her inner thigh. One of the men gives moist, enveloping kisses that form a timeless continuum; it would be simpler to just hibernate inside his mouth. The other's kisses are noncommittal, taunting little jabs that infuriate Clarice, especially as she has to stay passive to show no favouritism. While the outside of her is inert, there is hot, cataclysmic activity within her, in the unseen realm beneath her skin. Her poor skin bears the heavy task of concealment. But her belly is going warm, all of her turning as soft as the sheets.

Soon there is no hiding anything and she finds herself rolling from side to side like a fidgety insomniac. She is in a mounting torment of indecision. Who to turn to? Which touch to receive? It is too much, in the manner of a relentless savage tickling; she is beyond her own control.

Who is she trying to fool? One of the men has kept his hat on, but still, she has never been able to keep track of which is which; the one without a hat looks a little as Paul might have looked, had he grown up. Their caresses flow together, the two sets of hands complementing one another, touching, overlapping, behaving as a single pair of ubiquitous hands. She has never been touched like this, with no way out.

It is stuffy and hard to see from under her hair, which winds around her face. She is breathing roughly through her mouth, her legs slackening and falling further apart; this is probably shameful. The men are beginning to smile, as if unable to resist a joke much longer. She is ready to say, *enough*, or, *wait a minute*, but the two of them—him on the left and him on the right—are so well synchronised, like a ventriloquist and his dummy.

If the men complete one another so perfectly, what is

her role? Not knowing makes her anxious. Is she superfluous? The sea breeze lifts, the drapes, those airy slabs of sky, twitching violently.

Clarice comes back to her senses in a sweat, but the tension of the dream leaks quickly away. Her real bed is small, narrow, unembellished and very tightly tucked. She briefly thrashes her legs to loosen the constrained feeling; no luck for now, but she will try again later.

A couple of painters came once to speak to Meldrum's class about Asian art. They were a vivid pair, married but childless and just returned from a year in Japan that had made passionate Japanophiles of them. It was rumoured that they engaged in secret ceremonies they had learned over there, wearing just kimonos.

Dadie was the woman's name. She had long dark hair, stylish and possibly dyed, and you could tell that the time in Japan had made life seem enigmatic and precious to her; she was living in some trance. You could see her in a kimono. Clarice had forgotten the husband's name. He had had an allure similar to his wife's—a reserved enthralment—but was more austere and let her do the talking.

Dadie insisted on the importance of a Japanese word: *ma*. 'Loosely translated, it means something such as "pause" or "gap",' she elaborated, speaking as if gazing spellbound at a vista only recently revealed to her.

Someone had loudly interjected that *ma* meant *but* in Italian.

'Oh?' responded Dadie pleasantly, though she was on a path she could not be distracted from. 'Perhaps that's not unfitting.' *Ma*, she had gone on to explain, was employed to describe the use of empty space in the design of a garden— garden design being an art in its own right in Japan. 'The Japanese know the value of empty space.' Dadie paused to allow her words to shine through a bubble of emptiness. 'They recognise it as a crucial element of composition.'

Arthur was in that classroom, out of Clarice's view but not her sense of the moment. Remembering in her small, tight bed, ruffled by the dream, though gradually more serene, she thinks that it takes time to weigh this notion of *ma*, to give your blessing to its starkness. But of course empty space is sparkling, heartbreaking, sensual. It can be turned to your advantage.

32

There is a poor dear sitting on the far side of the solarium. She is nicely witchy, with noble, sloping bones and skin like creased silk. Someone has wrapped her in a sad, grey shawl. Red might have lifted her mood; a bit of red will do it. The old girl appears to be taken with the clouds, high and neat, that the windows frame.

Those clouds are white innocence. No intimation of rain. It is not that clouds are malicious or that they bluff; their intentions are changeable because their ideas are so transient. Over and over, they embody the slightest whim.

If Clarice were feeling a little stronger, she would talk to the woman, who looks old but could even be her own age. Forty-eight! Already getting on in years. She is not often at ease with strangers. Solitude is the artist's luxury, valuable currency— but as with any wealth, it is unadvisable to hoard. She is not uncomfortable in the old woman's presence, though. Maybe it is her air of not having long to go; a slackness around the mouth that could be the softening of fatigue or the start of a grin.

The redhead bustles in, paying no attention to the old girl. This is a restful thing about age, she supposes, the way it ushers you into invisibility, as though into the plush recess of a theatre booth.

The nurse asks, 'A piece of toast?'

While the redhead is certainly tough, she is not mean like Father's nurse. Really not persecutory at all. She has forgiven Clarice for rejecting lunch.

The redhead lowers her voice. '*Raisin* toast? Don't tell the others.'

Clarice is sorry to have no use for the secret.

'Soup? Cook made potato soup. You'll want something.'

She would not mind a cup of tea, actually. Good strong tea, milky. A generous dissolving cloud of milk—farm milk. It would take such an effort to ask.

'Just a slice of bread? I'll sprinkle sugar on it.'

'Not hungry.' Her voice comes and goes; you cannot always be polite and good—it is much easier once you have accepted this. The nurse's hand drops to Clarice's shoulder, like a travel-spent bird landing. That hand has a satisfying volume and an agreeably androgynous, bulky shape lit by shades of peach and mottled plum on the underside. She feels her own frailty beneath it and does not like it.

'Not even an apple?' the nurse whispers seductively. 'I'll cut it into pieces.'

Shaking her head causes a prickling in her rib cage. The redhead's face is still asking about the apple. Clarice attempts to assemble the components of a smile. This makes her cough and there is the sound: a chesty vibration, a faint whistling in the tree branches of her lungs; a thin, eerie wind. The muscles between her ribs feel bruised, overly human. An interesting way to cough, low, fundamental, the whole body a casualty. She leans back against the chair. It addles her that repose can be as tranquillising as work.

The hand on Clarice's shoulder moves back and forth, the bird anxious. 'You know, you'll come through this, the doc says. He's a great believer in mind over matter.'

The mention of a doctor gentles her, making her think of her own Doctor. 'So am I. The mind's potential is larger than our common idea of it.'

The redhead's eyebrows seem to have lifted, but not unkindly. Clarice smiles again, recalling the face of that old dear over by the window; she is a little worried for her.

33

Paul is elsewhere; you could not quite say where he is. Louise, the gloating, glowing one, is in the kitchen with Mum. Exultant accomplices, they are making peanut biscuits. The steep spirals of their laughter are as sweet and forbidden as the biscuits that are still cooking. If you do not wait till they are ready, the dough will make you sick.

But in the drawing room, in shadow, Rosamund, who is a doll but also an imposing princess, reclines in her bower that is regal with wattle and velvet ribbons—a shockingly vibrant vision, this, which Clarice has orchestrated.

'Puss. Puss!' She tempts Daffy forward with a twig.

Daffy's grey-flecked yellow eyes are ripe with cat madness. Spontaneous and calculated, she leaps into a pool of sun, like an actor into a spotlight. The rabbit trap might have taken her leg but not a whit of her spirit; cats have stupendous freedom in them.

Clarice, bored: 'Then the fairies floated cartwheeling to the top branch of the oak. The children did not realise the fairies were keeping watch over them. Louise skipped off along the bank of the Yarra, Clarice just behind . . .'

A little distracted, Rosamund and Daffy listen to the end of the latest episode of Mum's before-bed story. The doll and the cat love Clarice as crazily, as perfectly as Mum loves Louise.

When the Nocturne begins, Clarice understands that she is not in fact with Rosamund and Daffy, because that music came after and it has been a while, so long since the three friends were the points of a magic triangle.

34

She is not taken to the solarium.

Sleep washes tentatively against spiky islands of coughing. Breathing is a chore. Light slides across her sickroom trailing shadow, like the train of a gown; then it begins its late-afternoon metamorphosis. This moment—her evening work session approaching, the second daily reward of three hours—always lifts her. Because what she yearns for is close: soon she will be pulling her cart along the coast road.

Once or twice, the redhead tries to entice her with food. Clarice would oblige if she could, but appetite is one more emptied box. She gratefully accepts water from a cup, however. The doctor comes, listens to her chest and does some other things to which she does not pay much attention.

'I was here before,' Louise says. Her sister in the visitor's chair, beside the desiccating pinkish roses. 'I came the other day.'

'I know.'

'You're even paler than usual. Look at you.' Not managing to be humorous: 'Clarice's ivory skin.'

'You're wearing my bracelet.'

'This? Well, I've been staying at the house and I borrowed it. Anyway, you remember that time, with my jumper.'

'No, I've forgotten. I love the green in the glass bits. So I'll be wanting it back.'

'Makes you think of a fancy motor—the green.'

'It does. I'm going to need some things from home. My trolley. Some supplies. I'll make you a list. While I think of it, here's the key to the shed. Father can't be trusted with it.'

'He can't?'

'Absolutely not.'

'I'll take your word for it.'

'Good of you. Take that, too.'

'What's the second key?'

She feels panic. 'Take it.'

'Okay, okay.'

'It's for a bathing box.'

'A bathing box?'

'At Half Moon Bay. Go before Thursday.'

'Thursday. You're becoming demanding in your old age.'

'I am, but it's important, Louise. Please. You'll leave a note there for me. And a painting, won't you?'

'Oh God. A tryst?'

'You will, won't you?' She hears herself coming across as desperate.

'Calm down. I'll do whatever you want.'

'So. Are you shocked?'

'Not really.' Next to Louise, the roses are a paltry gesture at beauty; she puts them to shame.

'I imagined you'd be shocked.'

'Relieved, I think.'

'I'm not going to tell you who it is. It's not the Carruthers boy.'

'Suit yourself.' Louise laughs a little, appearing stricken. 'You're always secretive.'

'I know. I'm sorry. Well, no—not really. That's how I am. Louise?'

'Or how you decide to be. What? Don't tire yourself out.'

'I'm not tired now. How are you?'

'Fine.'

'Really?'

'You know.'

'The kiddies?'

'Troublemakers.' She smiles unevenly.

'You really do look a lot like Louise Brooks. You could be twins.'

'Do I? Still?' She sinks one hand into her glossy cropped hair and pouts. 'Everyone always used to tell me that.' Her face becomes sweet and sisterly.

One time as she sleeps, pressure on her bladder lends her dreams an erotic mood that does not seem to have anything to do with the dreamed events; it passes over them, a savoury odour on the wind, coming from someone else's cooking.

Collins Street. Her city is enfolded in mist, which she wears like a stole. She can make out the spiky silhouette of the Manchester Unity Building, that man-made mountain, its tower and spire triumphantly lit. There is no one else around to enjoy it. Good to be alone, though, finally. It is late. Her only city. All the things that others find unsightly are extra reasons for tenderness, as far as she is concerned, as would be the idiosyncrasies of an adored child.

Mouth open, she is tasting wood and coal smoke, a woman's perfume, the moist cold of a Melbourne night, its streamlined thinking in black, blue, purple, when a motorcar approaches from behind. She steps quickly out of the road and onto the footpath.

A girl, a woman. Olive of the summery frock and the twirling? It seems to be, but then she turns further and—how quickly one person can melt into someone else—it is Ada. Slim, almost a shadow. Her friend, Ada, peering out through the rear window into the motor's wake, as its refined, funereal form disappears.

She would like to stop the car and ask Ada one or two things. What has she been painting? It would be wrong for Ada to let her painting go, though so many do. Too late. Clarice waves, but cannot tell if Ada has seen her.

Woken by her throbbing bladder, she is mildly aroused. So full with that ache at her centre, replete, she delays ringing the bell on the nightstand. She lies there until she cannot postpone it. She rings. Depending on others is new and awkward, like borrowing a showy person's clothes. She rings again. The quiet suggests collective sleep, but subconscious adventures are a private matter, each dipping into his well. Or do all the wells draw from the same body of water?

The redhead. Yawning but amenable. 'Do you need the bedpan, love? Cold night, isn't it?' In the lamplight, her red hair sticks out, a charming coppery chaos of angles.

Clarice nods, sorry to have disturbed her. She was unaware of the cold, although they are halfway down the path of winter. She savours winter's austerity, the dramatic things it does to sky and skin, and hates to be away from the weather. Even when Mum was bad, near the end, she could steal the odd moment to lean against the garden fence and breathe. Her hands, then and now: hot, itchy and unhappy; not using them for painting makes her hands bereft.

She tinkles against the enamel, appreciating the nurse's tact. Her thighs are mauve-grey and unusually feeble. Those do not appear to be the legs that stride the streets of Beaumaris day after day, the legs grasped by the Doctor's hands. Are they really the same that have always held her up?

Her nightgown rearranged, she finds herself perched on the side of the hard little bed, as if she were her own visitor—sick Clarice's visitor. But no one is lying in the bed; there is a feeling of expectation, as though sick Clarice might soon return. She does not want her to.

The Clarice who is only visiting the ailing, absent Clarice sees the moon. Where the curtain does not meet the window frame, she recognises the midwinter moon, coyly incomplete, clouded. She is as dizzy as a girl.

'Could you please open the curtain?' she asks.

'What's that?'

'The curtain.' She shakily lifts her arm to mime pulling it across.

The redhead considers this. You would think looking at the moon was bad for the health. An old idea, no? The moon and madness.

There is a heavy thud. From which room it has come, Clarice is not sure; she cannot find the layout of this place in her memories. How many days is it since the storm? Some unlucky thing must have fallen out of bed. Low groaning follows the initial sound. The old woman from the solarium? She did not look sturdy and Clarice fears for her.

'Good gracious,' exclaims the nurse, resigned.

She hurriedly helps Clarice into bed, but—about to rush off—pauses and pulls the curtain aside.

Some time after, the redhead's consoling voice can be heard, far off.

Clarice calls, uneasily, 'Is she alright?'

No reply, but there are other sounds and she imagines the movements of limbs and mouths causing those vibrations—metallic, wooden, human—that cruise the air to her ears. The senses. She kicks at the tight sheet, then, weary, allows her focus to narrow. Now she listens only to the air coming in; a sort of ragged sucking on the inhalation. Her lungs are an accordion expanding and contracting, but the sound is of a humbler instrument. A rattle, a baby's half-broken rattle. Is this reflex, instinct?

But another breath and she treats herself to the strange

227

moon. The pleasure of it, more intense for having earlier been denied, makes her think her loneliness could be a form of union in disguise.

The sun pokes over the horizon. Globular and glistening. Like illicit lovers creeping back into clothes, the few gum trees she can make out ease stealthily into their daytime selves.

35

Though she has heard the name of this doctor on several occasions, it will not stick, so, copying the redhead, she calls him the doc. For fun, but also out of loyalty—to differentiate him from the Doctor. 'We'll have to try a bit harder,' the doc says. There is affection overflowing from this. He seems to be telling a circuitous joke, the punchline just around the corner; she cackles a little, sensing it, as a spiritualist might a presence on the other side. This levity has been coming in waves. 'Clarice,' he murmurs, brushing her stringy hair from her eyes.

Concern, in his face, and she must look a fright, but she has no use for mirrors. For some time, she has been lightening her load, dispensing with unnecessary burdens; there is an elegant simplicity to it. She has the impression— although it is not the case, for obvious reasons—that Mum is at the foot of the bed, attentively overseeing. Mum beams her approval, thrilled; she is kidding herself that Clarice might marry the doc. Marry, no, not this time around, but he is pleasantly quiet and methodical, his breath cleanly saline, maritime.

'In the last days,' Clarice finds herself saying, 'before my mother was bedridden, she had a funny way of walking around the house.' He leans close, nods. Now Clarice sees a later moment but does not describe it, the shape that Mum took as she was going, like a baby animal curled around a placenta, a seashell, a crescent moon.

The doc does not comment. Again, he moves her hair out of her eyes, off her forehead; it could be another man caressing her, expert, blissful hands and inscrutable motivations. She should probably say something appropriate, be reassuring, but there is an anarchic impulse building in her, some disobedience.

Clarice suffers, thinking of Half Moon Bay. She thrashes against the sheets, and finally there is a loosening, her legs are unbound.

The air has changed. She had taken this room at face value, taken it for a nursing-home room like any other; she judged it too quickly. She strains to lift herself onto her elbows, tilting her head like a dog struggling to identify a pattern in nonsense.

Something quite unusual is happening. Are the walls shimmering? She squints. Objects that moments before had names like *table* or *chair* now elude their names, which is as it should be; but they are also swimming free of their habitual moorings, their positions, tones and forms becoming unidentifiable. And colours are taking advantage of this situation to similarly defect from their countries of origin and generally horse around. It is all disintegrating in a horrifying or rather exciting way, turning abstract, awaiting reinvention.

The wild state of affairs shows her the secret nature of the room in which she is lying. It is not just any room, no—it is a studio. A space consecrated to art. With this realisation, the moody Nocturne starts up again. She curls and uncurls her fingers, limbering up. Impatient to be working, she consoles herself with the idea that she has already begun; the work, after all, is mainly seeing.

Olive is in the corridor, just beyond the doorway of the studio. Everything is apparently much as it always was, in the corridor, although it is possible the woman no longer calls herself Olive. Clarice wonders what is wrong with her, if she could be cured already; she looks in perfect health, chirpy even, but sometimes the problem is convincingly hidden.

'Hello,' mouths Olive, who is far from shy, bless her.

She has elaborately tangled hair. A string of fake-looking pearls cinches her neck, giving her a whiff of downtrodden glamour. What is strange about Olive? Those pearls? That she persists in underdressing for the weather—today sporting a light blouse and skirt? Her bare feet?

'Aren't you cold?' Clarice speaks loudly. She would like to invite Olive into the studio to get warm. 'I should really be going,' she says. 'There's something I have to do.' She is panting: it is like noticing you have begun to speak a foreign language, like giving up a portion of control. She fights it, asking herself what other roads there might be.

Olive turns to check no one is behind her. Quickly unbuttoning her blouse, she yanks it open to show Clarice the pallid hillock of her left breast.

'Oh.'

Olive is clearly the type of person who knows that art makes it all poetry, scrambling the lower with the higher things. She says, 'We don't get much to eat here. Luckily, I'm not very hungry,' winks and is gone.

'Neither am I.'

The wheezing calls for a visit, *Hello, me again*. But Clarice will not be distracted. She is remembering the lusty storm—the surprising smoky calm at its heart. She shivers. Her wet dress might still be moulded to her skin. She wishes she had her trolley or at least a nice piece of charcoal. As she is looking, eyelids almost lowered, for the darkest and the brightest regions, the redhead returns, as wondrous in the shadows as her old doll, Rosamund.

Hushing her: 'It's alright, love. It's alright.'

'Could you wait a minute?' she says, concentrating. 'I'm just getting somewhere.'

36

'It's going to rain,' the Doctor predicted, serenely analytical, looking through the door of the green bathing box that was a fraction ajar. A crisp wind darted in.

She was stooped over, with her back to him, lacing up her boots. 'It might.' She stood and inhaled. 'Yes, you're right. Not for a bit, but soon.'

It was her habit to wait for him in the bathing box at Half Moon Bay on Thursday afternoons. They had a ritual of arriving and leaving at different times, but it was June and they did not encounter many people on the little beach—and no one who, noticing them, had seemed to find anything awry. Perhaps they had just been lucky; they felt lucky—felt they were owed some luck—and this was the eccentric, captivating package it had arrived in.

He had given her the key to keep. It was like a ring between them, only less symmetrical and certain, more original and teasing. She loved the cold metal of it in the morning and also how quickly it warmed in her palm. Sometimes, just woken, she seized it from her bedside table, hoisted up her nightgown and laid their key on her stomach, flinching and then relaxing, observing how the loop at the end echoed her belly button. She adored having it in her pocket—its slight but important weight. She adored it on the kitchen counter, where it would have been difficult to explain, if someone had asked her to. The key was similar to having a drink in certain company, the way it sent out ripples, making everything pregnant and portentous, playfully grave.

There was no theatrical haste; waiting, she had very slowly, piece by piece, removed and folded her clothes, lingering in the partially undressed state, conscious of a pleasing sort of torpor. Thin beams of light—dusty, mollified winter light—insinuated themselves through gaps in the bathing box's wooden boards. The wind also occasionally forced its way in, singing spectrally. It was really much too cold at that time of year to be naked with only the meagre protection of rough uninsulated walls, but she relished the sense of hardship, of standing on an inhospitable frontier. She toyed with a pretend suspicion that someone was watching.

Her body in a loose focus. Perhaps she looked spare and modern, with her hair cut nearly as short as a boy's, though she knew she had reached an age where the beauty that had sometimes been remarked on was coming into doubt. It had not, after all, been innate and immovable. Its vestiges were still there, but these were more apparent some days than others. She caught a new shifting quality in her face, the rare times she consulted a mirror, a compelling hesitancy. Her eyes, Clarice liked to think, had become richer, more wakeful. And she approved of her hands. These were the only part of her you could not have called pale, and she was proud of their workmanlike colour. In the hut's penumbra, they seemed even darker, a little orange, and consequential. She held one up, shaking and blurry. She was trembling and not only from the cold. You had never finished with this heady, risky mix of fear and elation, the exhilarated panic; if anything, as time passed, the stakes got higher.

She felt him approaching. Here he came, piecing together a path to her. If she had anything, it was an awareness of how landforms, vegetation, weather, built things and men animated space, influencing its mood.

A noise, outside. In retrospect, she would understand it as the cry of a gull, oddly grating, wounded. She was startled. Her balance disturbed, she was suddenly tumbling into the wall of the bathing box. When her arm shot out to break her fall, her hand snagged on wood.

A splinter had pierced her skin and slipped under it; the shock was curiously smooth. She gasped, but barely made a sound and the violent non-sound made her think of the silent lovemaking that would follow. Her heart beat a touch off-kilter. The sensation in her palm throbbed between pain and itch. She did not remove the splinter, however. There was not much longer to wait. And perhaps anticipation was the most extravagant and affecting part of this.

She had begun to see sex as a particular kind of detail in a composition. It was a detail that could appear unassuming.

It might be small, half hidden, indefinite, and yet the surrounding space was in thrall to it, aware of an undertow. The space around sex was not empty—as sex was not without emptiness; sensuality was more and less than itself, nothing and everything, and in this way it resembled what could not be entirely seen in a painting.

He came in quickly. They did not say hello. Like a mannequin displaying an imaginary dress, she turned around for him.

Unselfconsciously but with a faint physical stiffness that seemed liturgical to Clarice, he undressed. She liked watching him. He was both stocky and soft, his body not athletic or beautiful. Her attraction to him hummed below the level of appearances.

A little sooner than she had expected, he approached her where she was standing by the wall. Her hand hurt and the wood behind her was furry, abrasive. Subdued light striped her skin, but he would not notice it. There was an odour of salt and burning tea-tree.

She spread her arms, comically sacrificial, offering herself. As she did so, he saw something, maybe in her lopsided smile, which his eyes were versed in.

'What's wrong?' he demanded.

She glanced at her pulsating hand.

'Show me that,' he said in his formal doctor's voice.

'You're going to paint in the rain?'

'Yes, of course.'

'You're not serious?' He might have been a little jealous of her art.

'I couldn't be more serious. It's wonderful to work in the rain.'

'I'm consorting with a madwoman.'

'You knew what you were getting into.'

'I did?'

'There are few things I enjoy more than painting in the rain. I'm offended you didn't know that, after all these weeks. How well do you know me?'

'Fair question,' he said. 'Ten weeks.'

Unusually—it was a decision they had reached by some tacit agreement—they left the bathing box together that evening. He drew her cart along, gallant and lightly vexed. They sat for a moment, half turned to the water, on the stone wall at the end of the beach.

She was staring at the *Cerberus*. The old armoured warship was partly visible above the very slight waves thirty yards or so out from shore, where it served as a breakwater. It was disturbingly incongruous-looking, like some queer submarine rising from the deep.

'The gun turrets are intact,' he said. They had been looking at the same thing.

'Oh?'

They studied the ship's darkening silhouette, tamed but still somehow threatening.

'Avant-garde eighteen-sixties technology.'

'The French refer to this time of day as the time between the dog and the wolf, *entre le chien et le loup*.'

'Pretty accent. Loathed French at school, myself. Say it again.'

'Maybe it's not so much the interval between the dog and the wolf,' she reflected, 'but of the change from one to the other. You know, the dog becoming the wolf.' She looked at him, then turned back to the bay. 'The words for this time are so poetic. Painfully so. *Twilight. Dusk*. Don't you think? *Crepuscular. Gloaming*. Gorgeous. Almost too beautiful.'

He did not snicker.

When she was ready, she told him, 'Get away with you now so I can work.'

'Can I help you take the cart somewhere?'

'I'll manage. Actually, this looks good from here. Adieu.' She laughed. She was not willing to miss a moment of this gentle final light, the soft implosion.

'Next Thursday, then?'

'Thursday.'

It did not take long for a churning muscular darkness swirled with pearl grey to come into view, approaching quickly. There was electricity in the air; you thought of séances, of bright messages flashing over and above any normal communication. One of them throbbing, her hands did seem possessed, as she made her preparations. She was only half thinking, vivid, unweighted thoughts. She felt almost light-headed but strong; she was going to paint her way right into the storm. Everything was splendid and as it had to be.

She did not really expect anyone to understand what she

was doing. The refreshing thing about being accustomed to disregard was the mighty freedom it allowed. It did not matter if the paintings in her next exhibition did not sell; that would not damage her. She would go on painting what and how she liked, and there was an end on it.

The work began well or rather, neither well nor badly, occupying a place cleansed of judgement. There was only the work doing itself, what it needed to do. The always-unexpected tricky moral, depth in the surface. When the rain came, she welcomed it wholeheartedly, angling her board and letting it close around her like drapes around privacy. Not fearing sopping clothes and bedraggled hair, savouring the deluge's first sweet drops, she slid into the calm rapture of her own transformation, her self dissolving. The clouds unveiled their inky plans, their violet and indigo inners, their luscious complexity. And the panel was thirsty, sucking in the paint that was spreading fast, silky with medium, just enough and just so.

Author's Note

The Clarice who appears in this work is not Clarice Beckett (1887–1935) but my imagining of her. While the historical figure's art and life inspired me, I took many creative liberties with these. The protagonist's family and personal life, for instance, are invented, as are the other characters— including Meldrum, another imagining of the historical figure whose surname he borrows. Among other facts, I have changed names, dates and places, and the art in these pages is also fictional: paintings were reinvented through language, altered and sometimes fabricated entirely; the dates of completion of several that correspond closely to works by Beckett differ considerably from those of the real works. I attempted to 'look' at Beckett as she might have looked at a landscape, squinting to soften edges and reach beyond detail in the search for patterns of light and shade.

The following books were extremely useful in my research: first and foremost, Rosalind Hollinrake's *Clarice Beckett, The Artist And Her Circle* and *Clarice Beckett:*

Politically Incorrect; Tracey Lock-Weir's *Misty Moderns: Australian Tonalists 1915–1950* and Max Meldrum's *The Science of Appearances*. *Nettie Palmer: her private journal 'Fourteen years', poems, reviews and literary essays*, edited by Vivian Smith, and Jeff Sparrow's *Communism: A Love Story* were also valuable reference points. The quote from Henry David Thoreau comes, of course, from *Walden*. The phrase likening the effect of Clarice's art to 'looking through an opening' was taken from a review in *The Age* by Alec Colquhoun of Beckett's 1927 exhibition.

The author gratefully acknowledges the assistance of the
University of Adelaide, the University of Western Sydney,
the Australian/Vogel Literary Award and Allen and Unwin.
Special thanks to Nicholas Jose, Rosalind and Ian Hollinrake,
Clara Finlay, Judith Lukin-Amundsen, Catherine Milne,
Siobhán Cantrill, the team at Goose Lane Editions, Jim Mott,
Jim Healy, Jeff Sparrow, James Eichelberger, Carl Nielsen,
Stephen Lawrence, Hazel Rowley, Moya Costello, Gail Jones,
Gary Thornell and Miguel Alonso.